SAINT MARY 365

Book 7

聖母に捧詩 365 節

Stean Anthony

YAMAGUCHI SHOTEN

Verse on the cover from:
"For the Mighty One has done great things for me,
and holy is his name.
His mercy is for those who fear him
from generation to generation."
"Mary's Song," Luke 1.49-50 NRSV

Hear my voice at:
<http://www35.tok2.com/home/stean2/>

SAINT MARY 365 BOOK SEVEN
© 2019 Stean Anthony
Author's profits
See end of book for details
PRINTED IN JAPAN

HUMBLY DEDICATED TO
OUR LADY OF AKITA

Saint Mary 365 Book Seven
Contents

Preface		17
Books and Websites Consulted		19
1.	Wisdomword 7: Wisdom calls to you	20
2.	神戸 Kōbe: Chaste sculpted portals	20
3.	Sainte Thérèse 1: Il a mis devant mes yeux le livre de la nature	20
4.	Candle Flower: The blue oxygen petal	21
5.	Cana: The third day the mother of Jesus was there	21
6.	Ancient British Saints 1: The long second hand hurries round	21
7.	Wisdomword 8: Look to the ant you lazy fool	22
8.	Church on the Nerli: Holy perfection this temple for God	22
9.	Sainte Thérèse 2: He opened before me the Book of Nature	22
10.	Tsubaki: From the corner of a Japanese garden	23
11.	Cyclamen: Pouring water on my head	23
12.	Ancient British Saints 2: There is time enough to live in	23
13.	Wisdomword 9: My child keep your father's word	24
14.	Adoration of the Child: Otherworldly are the distant lands	24
15.	Sainte Thérèse 3: In the living garden of the Lord	24
16.	Mary's Dowry: Anglia dos Mariae	25
17.	Winter Sweet: Fragrant yellow flowers	25
18.	Ancient British Saints 3: A great gulf of time behind us	25
19.	Wisdomword 10: Wisdom is my sister	26
20.	Maternità: I shall be mother	26
21.	Sainte Thérèse 4: Swiftly the sunny years of childhood	26
22.	Rose Window Saint-Malo: Nine saints niches flowers for God	27
23.	Marathon School: In the gateway she appears	27
24.	Ancient British Saints 4: Walk with me the ancient spirits	27
25.	Wisdomword 11: Little ones do not be foolish	28
26.	Saint Luke & Virgin: Luke writes the icon	28
27.	Sainte Thérèse 5: You were always there to kiss me awake	28
28.	Folk Dress: The snow thaws the river released	29
29.	胡坐 Agura: My ankles crossed I perch	29
30.	Ancient British Saints 5: Family fighting family	29
31.	Wisdomword 12: All my words are right	30
32.	Candlemas: The candlestick	30
33.	Sainte Thérèse 6: Happy days when my dear king	30

34.	Where's this? 23: Alphonsa stand in a sentry box	31
35.	Made Man: Back to the dawn of my life again	31
36.	Ancient British Saints 6: Pray for me Saint Columba	31
37.	Wisdomword 13: The fear of the Lord	32
38.	Irène: Brushing through her auburn hair	32
39.	Sainte Thérèse 7: On the day of first communion	32
40.	Where's this? 24: In your remembrance Colman	33
41.	Mary & Jesus: Mother running after me	33
42.	Ancient British Saints 7: Iona beacon in the darkness	33
43.	Wisdomword 14: By me kings reign in justice	34
44.	柿 Sharon Fruit: Astringent in the memory	34
45.	Sainte Thérèse 8: Listen my little Queen, your patron saint	34
46.	Mariazell Basilica 1: With your eye	35
47.	Word Flower 5: Sounds like a swift descent	35
48.	Ancient British Saints 8: Take your shoes off and feel the sand	35
49.	Wisdomword 15: The Lord brought me forth as the first	36
50.	Two Sisters: Ma mère régarde à la rivière	36
51.	Sainte Thérèse 9: On my way home I would gaze at the stars	36
52.	Mariazell Basilica 2: Father wore blue sky and sun	37
53.	Holy Trinity Icon: There are three angels at the table	37
54.	Ancient British Saints 9: King Oswald called me from Iona	37
55.	Wisdomword 16: I was there when he set the heavens in place	38
56.	Christ Appearing: Young boy kneeling in the highlands	38
57.	Sainte Thérèse 10: That same evening as the sun set	38
58.	Joachim & Anna: Before Jerusalem the Golden Gate	39
59.	Akashi: Spirit on the waters in the early morning	39
60.	Ancient British Saints 10: Monks on a raft swept down the Tyne	39
61.	Wisdomword 17: I was constantly at His side	40
62.	Mother of God Enthroned: The anointed king	40
63.	Sainte Thérèse 11: Riven with trauma and suffering	40
64.	Postage Stamp: Infant Jesus turning	41
65.	Flower in Season: It was a sunny day	41
66.	Ancient British Saints 11: Alone on the island of Inner Farne	41
67.	Wisdomword 18: Blessed are you who keep my ways	42
68.	Pardonne-leur: Born on the altar	42
69.	Sainte Thérèse 12: She appeared so lovely, so tender	42
70.	紅椿 Red Camellia: Flower little lily in the garden	43
71.	Daffodil 1: My beloved before thee I kneel	43

72.	Ancient British Saints 12: A bright angelic light in his face	43
73.	Wisdomword 19: Wisdom has built her house with seven pillars	44
74.	Pontmain Basilica: My spirit was dry like baked earth	44
75.	Sainte Thérèse 13: Marie asked me and I told her	44
76.	Cycladic: Stand in front of the glass	45
77.	Daffodil 2: My head on the earth	45
78.	Ancient British Saints 13: My holy relics were moved to Durham	45
79.	Wisdomword 20: The fear of the Lord is the beginning	46
80.	山百合 Yamayuri 2: Not a wand but an armful	46
81.	Sainte Thérèse 14: I was preparing for my first communion	46
82.	Anchor 1: Paying out the anchor chain	47
83.	Icon S.M. del P.: Mary my Mother	47
84.	Ancient British Saints 14: That it not lead to biffin	47
85.	Wisdomword 21: A wise daughter makes a glad father	48
86.	L'Annunciazione: Alarm bells are ringing	48
87.	Sainte Thérèse 15: In my heart the first kiss of Jesus	48
88.	Anchor 2: The anchor runs through the pawl	49
89.	Roettgen Pietà: The pain is over	49
90.	Ancient British Saints 15: The young man is singing a hymn	49
91.	Wisdomword 22: Here is a good word Love covers all offenses	50
92.	Good Friday: After the storm on Galilee subsided	50
93.	Easter Day: I will not say what it meant then	50
94.	Resurrection Icon: Under your feet the broken tomb	51
95.	When: I asked the weatherman	51
96.	Ancient British Saints 16: At the age of sixteen	51
97.	Wisdomword 23: The city prospers when you bless	52
98.	Christ Appears: Young boy kneeling in the highlands	52
99.	Sainte Thérèse 16: I would climb up to the tribune and wait	52
100.	Orthodox Kenya: The voice rises up to heaven	53
101.	Crab Apple: Can I remember you?	53
102.	Ancient British Saints 17: As I began to pray the world changed	53
103.	Wisdomword 24: The righteous are kind to their animals	54
104.	Boxing: Stand on guard my little one	54
105.	Sainte Thérèse 17: A picture of the crucifixion slipped out	54
106.	連翹 Rengyō: Pure childhood yellow	55
107.	Sit & Pray 1: Why do you sit cross-legged	55
108.	Ancient British Saints 18: Clear signs I was given to go back	55
109.	Wisdomword 25: A daughter loves her father's discipline	56

110.	Santa Maria del Popolo: The scallop above the doorway	56
111.	Sainte Thérèse 18: His cry as he died "I thirst" echoed	56
112.	Sister Cook: Sushi board dance to the Lord	57
113.	Sit & Pray 2: Sat upon the air above the flower	57
114.	Ancient British Saints 19: Sailed in a curragh the corner	57
115.	Wisdomword 26: A wise woman builds her house	58
116.	Spezzano Albanese: Our Lady give healing by Jesus	58
117.	Sainte Thérèse 19: Our hearts light we followed him	58
118.	Kurara 1: Pale-yellow bells	59
119.	Sit & Pray 3: Children on our visit today please note	59
120.	Ancient British Saints 20: He took you for the Mother Mhuire	59
121.	Wisdomword 27: The prayers of the upright delight the Lord	60
122.	Virgin with Milk: The window is the mind	60
123.	Sainte Thérèse 20: In the evening Céline & I in the belvedere	60
124.	Rosary on the Coast: They will be saying the rosary on Iona	61
125.	Flower of the Field: Winning bread, clothing the kids	61
126.	Ancient British Saints 21: Fleeing the wicked King they left	61
127.	Wisdomword 28: The path of the wise leads upward	62
128.	Our Lady of Lebanon: Round we go and round we go	62
129.	Sainte Thérèse 21: Switzerland! Towering mountains	62
130.	British Woodsman: I squeeze through the narrow trail	63
131.	Saint Xenia of Kalamata: Appeared as I prayed a blond angel	63
132.	Ancient British Saints 22: Cross of the Scriptures to teach me	63
133.	Wisdomword 29: A wise son delights his father	64
134.	Wheatgrass: A blue plate of light-brown wheat	64
135.	Sainte Thérèse 22: Loreto! This House sheltered	64
136.	Where's This 25: Saint Mary in Assumption	65
137.	Our Lady of Altötting: A gold cape with a red velvet table	65
138.	Ancient British Saints 23: Oats seethed in warm milk	65
139.	Wisdomword 30: Humility goes before honor	66
140.	Coaster: Messages found in curious places	66
141.	Sainte Thérèse 23: With special permission the priest said Mass	66
142.	Valaam Icon 1: My old body racked with pain	67
143.	Myrrh 1: Murmur to thee my little boy	67
144.	Ancient British Saints 24: I remember Ireland	67
145.	Wisdomword 31: Commit to the Lord	68
146.	Our Lady of Help 1: A blazon of golden rays behind her	68
147.	Sainte Thérèse 24: Speak whispered Céline. I knelt before him	68

148.	Our Lady of Help 2: Praying on my knees in the pew	69
149.	Bede's Prayer: O Christ, our Morning Star	69
150.	Ancient British Saints 25: Lessons to survival how he gave	69
151.	Wisdomword 32: When a king's face brightens	70
152.	Sacra Famiglia: Dancing on her hands	70
153.	Sainte Thérèse 25: O Très Saint Père, si vous disiez oui	70
154.	Rest on the Flight to Egypt: We are resting by the cool rocks	71
155.	Valaam Icon 2: O suffering mother little Russian saint	71
156.	Ancient British Saints 26: Still holding out your stiff arm	71
157.	Wisdomword 33: A friend loves at all times	72
158.	Valaam Icon 3: In red imperial gown	72
159.	Sainte Thérèse 26: Sainte Madeleine de Pazzi in Florence	72
160.	Igorevskaya Icon: Mother look from heaven	73
161.	Krakowiak 2: Ponies prancing round we go	73
162.	Ancient British Saints 27: Patient in stillness breathing	73
163.	Wisdomword 34: The name of the Lord is a strong tower	74
164.	Water Shrew: In the water again before you blink	74
165.	Sainte Thérèse 27: From Florence to Pisa to Genoa	74
166.	Dance for Mary 1: Performing the sword dance	75
167.	Mother Icon: From the gown her pearly arm	75
168.	Ancient British Saints 28: Pray for me Saint Kevin	75
169.	Wisdomword 35: When you are good to the poor	76
170.	青花 Aobana: The morning dew	76
171.	Sainte Thérèse 28: Father was planning a pilgrimage	76
172.	Dance for Mary 2: Light upon my toes springing	77
173.	浦島草 Urashimasō 1: Corona a wreath of golden-green	77
174.	Ancient British Saints 29: Fame of the Irish in the world	77
175.	Wisdomword 36: The Lord gives light to the human spirit	78
176.	Book of Kells 1: Lapis Lazuli blue and indigo	78
177.	Sainte Thérèse 29: My dream of life in the Carmel!	78
178.	Dance for Mary 3: In the air I float for thee	79
179.	Kurara 2: Sapphire wings with splotches	79
180.	Ancient British Saints 30: Where fair he taught let love be	79
181.	Wisdomword 37: A good name is better than wealth	80
182.	Book of Kells 2: Witness to the Irish we live	80
183.	Sainte Thérèse 30: The cross the way to win souls	80
184.	Passion Flower 1: I turned to the flower	81
185.	Rose en Sucre: Watch the clever fingers	81

10

186.	Ancient British Saints 31: Open the fush said Mungo	81
187.	Wisdomword 38: Apply your mind to instruction	82
188.	Book of Kells 3: Saints on the edge of the world	82
189.	Sainte Thérèse 31: The treasures of his face	82
190.	Passion Flower 2: I turned to the flower	83
191.	上海飴細工 Shanghai Amezaiku: A pan of brown sugar	83
192.	Ancient British Saints 32: Son of a prince gifted in speech	83
193.	Wisdomword 39: The vineyard was overgrown with thorns	84
194.	Marinera Nortena 1: Look how they dance upon the breeze	84
195.	Sainte Thérèse 32: He found a way of shaking hands	84
196.	Passion Flower 3: So let it flower	85
197.	Mother Sculpture: We made bricks from the earth	85
198.	Ancient British Saints 33: Not a story to make you laugh	85
199.	Wisdomword 40: If your enemies hunger, give them bread	86
200.	Marinera Nortena 2: Beautiful the feet upon the mountains	86
201.	Sainte Thérèse 33: A bridal gown with diamonds and jewels	86
202.	Fairy Reel: Heels and toes before and after	87
203.	Snowy Egret: Walking in the uplands	87
204.	Ancient British Saints 34: Margaret mother of Henry built thee	87
205.	Wisdomword 41: Do not boast about tomorrow	88
206.	Inca Dance: Under the white	88
207.	Sainte Thérèse 34: Desperate to know my vocation false	88
208.	Puhtitsa: A summer day procession	89
209.	DC-3 Design 1: Cut the aesthetics free	89
210.	Ancient British Saints 35: In the Idylls I crowned the king	89
211.	Wisdomword 42: Do not bless a friend with a loud voice early	90
212.	Saint Alphonsa: Powerful healer	90
213.	Sainte Thérèse 35: I pronounced my sacred vows	90
214.	Feria de las Flores: She strapped on the silleta	91
215.	DC-3 Design 2: He never intended you for that	91
216.	Ancient British Saints 36: Find me in the ancient name	91
217.	Wisdomword 43: The wise quietly restrain anger	92
218.	Irish Stamp: A word from Clare	92
219.	Sainte Thérèse 36: The story of the little flower	92
220.	提灯 Chōchin: They were carrying paper lanterns	93
221.	Mary Dancing: Dance my daughters	93
222.	Ancient British Saints 37: My relics divided miraculously	93
223.	Wisdomword 44: Who has gone up to heaven and come down	94

224.	Querrien: In the water of the holy spring there it is	94
225.	Lily: Bronze pillars with lilies	94
226.	Br. Junipero: Kneel by her picture	95
227.	Clare Procession: The brass band blares a joyful blast	95
228.	Ancient British Saints 38: 2000 years on my back	95
229.	Wisdomword 45: The tiny ant gathers her food in the summer	96
230.	Walsingham Well: Water from the well drink with my blessing	96
231.	Assumption: Twelve apostles stand amazed	96
232.	Mari Txindoli: Mother of the Vascones	97
233.	多羅葉 Tarayō: Broad lustrous oval leaves	97
234.	Ancient British Saints 39: The Lord in the saints shouts	97
235.	Wisdomword 46: Can you find a word of wisdom here	98
236.	Lithops: I was outside the walls	98
237.	Little Way 1: I will find a little way to heaven	98
238.	Carob: In the shade of the grateful tree	99
239.	Clareclown: Red stripy vest and giant shoes	99
240.	Ancient British Saints 40: In the darkness of the coal-black	99
241.	Wisdomword 47: Who can find a virtuous woman?	100
242.	Embroider: Blessed Virgin Holy Theotokos	100
243.	Little Way 2: I searched the Scriptures for a hint	100
244.	Kurara 3: Whispers a cold wind	101
245.	Resolute: Jesus set his face toward Jerusalem	101
246.	Ancient British Saints 41: Padstow from Petrocstow	101
247.	Wisdomword 48: She does him good	102
248.	Festa della Rificolona: In honor of our Mother's birth	102
249.	Little Way 3: Preferring this and disliking that	102
250.	Teresa Film: Almost fifty years since that famous film	103
251.	St Rose of Viterbo: On fire for God in the first word she spoke	103
252.	Ancient British Saints 42: Where your tomb is found	103
253.	Wisdomword 49: The merchant galley on the seas	104
254.	Our Lady of Mantara: We sealed up the entrance with rocks	104
255.	Little Way 4: We were washing clothes in the laundry	104
256.	Zampoña: Breathe a soft & rapid note	105
257.	Cirrocumulus: Majesty slept in the hills	105
258.	Ancient British Saints 43: From Ireland with companions	105
259.	Wisdomword 50: She chooses a field and buys it	106
260.	Kurara 4: The larvae build the house	106
261.	Little Way 5: I want Jesus to draw me into the flames of His love	106

12

262.	Akita Harvest: Riding the wind over Akita	107
263.	Palmyra: Chop away the outer	107
264.	Ancient British Saints 44: Sing out the names rejoicing	107
265.	Wisdomword 51: Her work profits the house	108
266.	Jakarta Dances: Little flowers dance for Paul	108
267.	Little Way 6: Mother Anne of Jesus who founded Carmel	108
268.	Hulling Rice: Mother is wearing a red sari	109
269.	Villager Dances: Saint Paul sister standing close	109
270.	Ancient British Saints 45: Britons to the Bretons	109
271.	Wisdomword 52: She reaches out to the poor	110
272.	Alexandrian Muscat: Cool breeze in the vineyard at seven	110
273.	Little Way 7: I will show you yet a better way	110
274.	Yam: Read it backwards	111
275.	Novitiate Dances: Four sisters in the sunshine	111
276.	Ancient British Saints 46: One of the seven Breton saints	111
277.	Wisdomword 53: Her clothing is fine linen and purple	112
278.	Solemn Profession: They plant a Madonna on Carmel	112
279.	Meaning of Icons 23: Theology and iconography	112
280.	Earth Fruits: Knobbly eyed indomitable	113
281.	Hāḍar Citron: Teachers explain	113
282.	Ancient British Saints 47: A pilgrim on the Tro Breizh	113
283.	Wisdomword 54: Strength and dignity are her clothing	114
284.	Our Lady of Good Help 1: Vision in my life	114
285.	Meaning of Icons 24: As we stand before the iconostasis	114
286.	Our Lady: To and fro the rally goes	115
287.	Our Lady of Good Help 2: There was no money	115
288.	Ancient British Saints 48: With my psalter honed sharp	115
289.	Wisdomword 55: Praise her for the work of her hands	116
290.	Our Lady of Good Help 3: Mary pioneered in Wisconsin	116
291.	Meaning of Icons 25: Raise your eyes to the Deisis	116
292.	Walk to Mary 1: I closed my eyes	117
293.	Walk to Mary 2: From St Joseph in Green Bay	117
294.	Ancient British Saints 49: From the British to the Bretons	117
295.	Wisdomword 56: Honor your mother as long as she lives	118
296.	St Peter of Alcantara: An hour or two of sleep per day	118
297.	Meaning of Icons 26: The image and the likeness of God	118
298.	Where's this? 26: Standing beneath a coconut tree	119
299.	Nyiur: Bless thy head	119

300.	Ancient British Saints 50: The name Léon may derive	119
301.	Wisdomword 57: Give charity my child	120
302.	Eel: Bury my head	120
303.	Meaning of Icons 27: Mandorla the Icon of the Sign	120
304.	Duke Humfrey: Flowering window	121
305.	Name Again 14: Do not go to their cities	121
306.	Ancient British Saints 51: A monk from Wales	121
307.	Wisdomword 58: Do to no one what you yourself hate	122
308.	大根 Daikon: To the blue height there is no cloud	122
309.	Meaning of Icons 28: Hodigitria She who guides	122
310.	Oils: Camphor to soothe and loosen	123
311.	Name Again 15: Mary dances with a tambourine	123
312.	Ancient British Saints 52: Nephew of Brieuc	123
313.	Wisdomword 59: Seek counsel from the wise	124
314.	Kalimantan Dance: Little Marys in white	124
315.	Meaning of Icons 29: Notice her eyes and long neck	124
316.	Zoom Out: The angel took me up	125
317.	Name Again 16: From Hebrew we change into Greek	125
318.	Ancient British Saints 53: Mighty in name long-haired	125
319.	Wisdomword 60: Give thanks to God	126
320.	What's the Saint's Name? Waiting eagerly for the kingdom	126
321.	Meaning of Icons 30: Can you tell the difference	126
322.	Gate Bridge: Lift up your heads	127
323.	Name Again 17: You take the yoke from my shoulders	127
324.	Ancient British Saints 54: Word of their ferocity dismayed me	127
325.	Wisdomword 61: A king's secret be kept	128
326.	Palm Oil 1: God's hands gave us the palms	128
327.	Meaning of Icons 31: Hodigitria transformed	128
328.	Akashi Bridge: Little one dream	129
329.	Name Again 18: Why do they spell it like	129
330.	Ancient British Saints 55: God mi gard she sang in Frank	129
331.	Wisdomword 62: Raphael said, No need to fear	130
332.	Palm Oil 2: Steel cylinder with eyes	130
333.	Meaning of Icons 32: The Mother seated in majesty	130
334.	Meganebashi: We are bridge builders you and I	131
335.	Name Again 19: The name & saw it was good	131
336.	Ancient British Saints 56: First Christian king	131
337.	Wisdomword 63: Praise the Lord for his goodness	132

14

338.	Our Lady of Charity 1: Blessed Virgin Mary on the sea	132
339.	Meaning of Icons 33: Mercy herself is transfigured	132
340.	Kimono: It was the monthly visit	133
341.	Name Again 20: 母音 Mary help me say	133
342.	Ancient British Saints 57: Baptized with Edwin by Paulinus	133
343.	Wisdomword 64: What has been is what will be	134
344.	Poinsettia: Felt better for you	134
345.	Meaning of Icons 34: Vladimir thy holy Russian icon	134
346.	Colonna dell Immacolata: Four prophets defend	135
347.	Our Lady of Charity 2: The great aureole	135
348.	Ancient British Saints 58: Gentle Caedmon sing of God	135
349.	Wisdomword 65: Better is the end than the beginning	136
350.	Red Rose: Give me a rose, a red rose for love	136
351.	Meaning of Icons 35: Meditate on the inner beauty	136
352.	Chamor: Are you a wild donkey	137
353.	St Daniel the Stylite: Solid square tower 12 m high	137
354.	Ancient British Saints 59: Forty days I fasted & blessed	137
355.	Wisdomword 66: Wisdom overflows like the Pishon	138
356.	Star Aniseed: Put it straight in my pot	138
357.	Meaning of Icons 36: Every line signifies fullness	138
358.	Piers Plowman 2: Truth tells us love is heavenly treacle	139
359.	Buy a Hat: How about white, tall and pointy?	139
360.	Ancient British Saints 60: Heavenly song descended	139
361.	Wisdomword 67: The image of the invisible God	140
362.	Where's this? 27: Three candles hold a Xmas flame	140
363.	Festivitas Natalis: All unaware on an afternoon	140
364.	Christmas 1: Did you hear what I heard	141
365.	Christmas 2: The moo cow took a good look	141
366.	Christmas 3: Narrow frame a myrtle-wreath	141
367.	Christmas 4: Look upon the good	142
368.	Christmas 5: The chiaroscuro of the mind	142
369.	Bara Brith: What shall we give the babe in the manger?	142
370.	St Stephen Icon: Behold, I see the heavens opened up	143
371.	Piers Plowman 3: Heaven could not hold him so heavy he were	143
372.	Ancient British Saints 61: Owen threw himself upon the ground	143
373.	Ancient British Saints 62: Daughter of Holy Saxon kings	144
374.	Ancient British Saints 63: Bede to bid command and pray	144
375.	Naoko 2: For all who read my verse	144

376.	Biscuit Song: Tin of biscuits I will share them	145
377.	Sunrise: Look at the dawn in the sky	145
378.	Four Angel Verses	146
379.	Maya	148
380.	Saint Joseph at Dawn	150
381.	Kimono	151
382.	Final Profession	152
383.	Walsingham Procession	153
384.	The Ecumenical Covenant (Sept 2018)	154

Notes on the Poems	156
Profile	167
Author's Profits	168
Word of Blessing	169
Books by Stean Anthony	170

Preface

This is volume seven of my anthology of poems and prayers to Saint Mary, Mother of Jesus, called also the Holy Mother, Theotokos, drawing on all traditions. The purpose is irenical. In the passage of time, from the resurrection of Christ to the present day, Christians split apart with bitterness and acts of war, forming a multitude of separate churches. Good people were martyred. The wounds of history remain. How can there be healing? If we think hard and look to tomorrow, we realize that we must love one another more. The world gets colder, in the rich nations few people care about faith. We need to grow closer. May the churches sit together at one table again! Healing will only be found through love and forgiveness, and by compromise for the sake of love. Thinking on this, I decided that I must change. As I went forward, I dedicated myself to the Holy Mother, to serve God by making books to teach the beauty of holiness that is in her, to share that beauty, and to make a gift for the whole world, visiting the Holy Catholic, Holy Russian, Holy Greek and other churches – seeking where she has been known. As a Christian I can say,

HELPMEGOD
TOPRAYBETTERTOYOU
ANDTHROUGHJESUS&MARY
HELPMETOLOVEYOU
ANDALLPEOPLE
BETTEREACH
DAYAMEN

The book is arranged as a calendar so that it may be read day by day, or consulted for particular days. I hope that it may be a good instrument to use to improve English ability (especially in nations where English is the second language), and also to stimulate interest in Mary, the Holy Mother. It is a companion volume to *Saint Mary 100* (Yamaguchi Shoten), an anthology of verses based on the Bible.

These poems are my own interpretations of the sources I have consulted. I have tried to give voice to the truth that I understood, but the reader must note that these are poems – (sometimes quotation and prayer as well, like small icons). For literary purposes I sometimes adapt – to make a point or a good phrase. Go to the original materials to discover more.

You will find a Saint Clare theme in this book (especially in August). This continues from my earlier books. My wish is to promote solidarity and strength between the Clares (Franciscan Sisters) and the Orthodox Sisters, to build love and strength for the Holy Mother.

In Book 7 there is an icon theme, a series for Saint Thérèse of Lisieux, and a series of Ancient British Saints, as well as continuing verses on other themes. Verses are more puzzling than before.

Websites & Books Consulted

Bede. *A History of the English Church and People.* Trans. Leo Sherley-Price. London: Penguin, 1968.

Saint Thérèse of Lisieux. *The Story of a Soul: The Autobiography of The Little Flower. (L'histoire d'une ame).* Ed. Mother Agnes of Jesus. Trans. Michael Day. Tan Books, 2010.

I have consulted a wide range of websites.

20

1   Jan 1   Wisdomword 7

Wisdom calls to you
I will tell you who I am
Hear my word of instruction
I will pour out my spirit upon you
I will make known my words to you.

Mary for peace with Islam! الله

2   Jan 2   神戸   Kōbe

Chaste sculpted portals
Light brown pillars
Waving green flags
In due season
Sweetness from heaven.

3   Jan 3   Sainte Thérèse 1

Il a mis devant mes yeux le livre de la nature
Toutes les fleurs créées par Lui sont belles
L'éclat de la rose et la blancheur du lys
Le parfum de la petite violette
La simplicité ravissante de la pâquerette.

4   Jan 4   Candle Flower
The blue oxygen petal
Lifts the dull orange
The dancing yellow
A gift of gravity
It's a blue sphere in space.

5   Jan 5   Cana
The third day the mother of Jesus was there
Jesus and his disciples also
The mother said, they have no wine
Jesus said to her, Woman! Not yet my hour
The mother to the servants, Do what he tells you to do.

6   Jan 6   Ancient British Saints 1
The long second hand hurries round
Is this the last minute of time
Seas rising land quaking
The fabric of the earth and sky
Tearing open the eternal dimension.

7   Jan 7   Wisdomword 8

Look to the ant you lazy fool
How she gathers her food
Happy in the harvest
How long will you lie abed
Will you not rise and get to work?

Mary for peace with Islam! الله

8   Jan 8   Church on the Nerli

Holy perfection this temple for God
Three tall arches the height of the walls
A single dome on a perfect square
In the water beside the house reflected
God-beloved Russia to heaven in thee.

9   Jan 9   Sainte Thérèse 2

He opened before me the Book of Nature
All the flowers He made are beautiful
The splendor of the rose, the whiteness of the lily
The perfume of the small violet
The ravishing simplicity of the daisy.

10   Jan 10   Tsubaki
From the corner of a Japanese garden
Tsubaki half opens her mouth
A golden voice
My child you are perfectly good
Grow strong in wisdom and God's love.

11   Jan 11   Cyclamen
Pouring water on my head
Thinking on the cyclamen
The flowers are serpents
Or descending angels
Is that writing on the leaves?

12   Jan 12   Ancient British Saints 2
There is time enough to live in
Time enough to remember
Cast back the mind
Gather again the sacrifices
Brothers & sisters gave their lives.

13   Jan 13   Wisdomword 9

My child keep your father's word
Follow your mother's advice
Bind them to your heart
Let them lead you
They are a lamp and a light.

Mary for peace with Islam! الله

14   Jan 14   Adoration of the Child

Otherworldly are the distant lands
In a flowering garden Mary prays
Veiled in gossamer
The Holy Word
The Church stands & angels hold her train.

15   Jan 15   Sainte Thérèse 3

In the living garden of the Lord
The great saints are lilies and roses
The little saints are daisies
Happy to delight Him as he looks
Happy to be as he wills and perfect this way.

16   Jan 16   Mary's Dowry
Anglia dos Mariae
King Richard sings in Latin
Heaven crowds to the window
The angel holds the red cross high
England be blessed the dowry of Mary.

17   Jan 17   Winter Sweet
Fragrant yellow flowers
The winter left her sunlight there
Hungry in the end of winter
I nibbled the buds and flowers
The perfume rose within me.

18   Jan 18   Ancient British Saints 3
A great gulf of time behind us
Yet we can still find bones
Scratched runes on wood
Words that speak of other ways
Water in the deep well echoes my song.

19   Jan 19   Wisdomword 10

Wisdom is my sister

Understanding is my friend

I will write your words on my heart

With my fingers I will number them

I will keep you as the apple of my eye.

Mary for peace with Islam! الله

20   Jan 20   Maternità

I shall be mother

Feeding thee

Tenderness is Love

Fed by thee

I shall be infant.

21   Jan 21   Sainte Thérèse 4

Swiftly the sunny years of childhood

Father would take us to the pavilion

Mother came with us on Sunday walks

Wheat fields with poppies and cornflowers

Far distances, wide spaces and tall trees.

22   Jan 22   Rose Window Saint-Malo
Nine saints niches flowers for God
The glory rose above
In the early hours
He woke the flowers
Peace in the light that fills the church.

23   Jan 23   Marathon School
In the gateway she appears
To the gold medal runs
A good pace
Open road at page one
Read in Greek & read again.

24   Jan 24   Ancient British Saints 4
Walk with me the ancient spirits
The woodland nymphs and sprites
The gods we hoped for now we find
God gave the world and all our time
All the stories begin with Him.

28

25   Jan 25   Wisdomword 11

Little ones do not be foolish
Be prudent and gain sense
Do not be so dull-witted
I will give you noble things
Wisdom will speak goodness.

Mary for peace with Islam! الله

26   Jan 26   Saint Luke & Virgin

Luke writes the icon
Mary with the infant
The brush
Is holy
To the smallest stroke.

27   Jan 27   Sainte Thérèse 5

You were always there to kiss me awake
I said my prayers kneeling beside you
You gave me a reading lesson
The first word I read was *heaven*
Then I went to see Father in the belvedere.

28   Jan 28   Folk Dress
The snow thaws the river released
A yellow apron of sun
Blue sky
Blessed white clouds
Daisies like promises of summer

29   Jan 29   胡坐   Agura
My ankles crossed I perch
The demons groan uncross
Earth your feet they curse
My mind I clear and pray
Mother Mary sit with me today.

30   Jan 30   Ancient British Saints 5
Family fighting family
Give life to the number of souls
As the number who died in the conflict
Be a dove   Iona   thou holy dovecot!
The soft voices sing in the sound of the sea.

30

31   Jan 31   Wisdomword 12

All my words are right
Take my instruction instead of silver
My knowledge rather than fine gold
Wisdom is better than rubies
Nothing you desire compares with me.

Mary for peace with Islam! الله

32   Feb 1   Candlemas

The candlestick
The woven wick
The living flame
Thy body thy soul thy divinity
The light of the world.

33   Feb 2   Sainte Thérèse 6

Happy days when my dear king
Took me fishing with him
I would sit in the flowery meadow
Lost in thought   without knowing
My soul was in a deep prayer to God.

34   Feb 3   Where's this? 23
Alphonsa stand in a sentry box
An angel in a window
You have to marry a rich man
I danced on the burning
I was fervent in love for Christ.

35   Feb 4   Made Man
Back to the dawn of my life again
Waiting in darkness
Outside is a tomb
Here I am in a cave
I will rise outward and bring heaven

36   Feb 5   Ancient British Saints 6
Pray for me Saint Columba
Bless my writing hand
Bless the bardic powers
Bless my prayer to Mary
Bless the family before and after, amen.

32

37   Feb 6   Wisdomword 13
The fear of the Lord
This is to hate what is evil
Pride and arrogance
Bad speaking
Cast these away from you.

Mary for peace with Islam! الله

38   Feb 7   Irène
Brushing through my auburn hair
Mother I love you
Unruly heart goes here and there
Thoughts go everywhere
But now my hair shines brightly.

39   Feb 8   Sainte Thérèse 7
On the day of first communion
Your prayers will be answered
So I prayed for the poor old man
It was many years later
Our Lord surely heard my prayer.

40   Feb 9   Where's this? 24
In your remembrance Colman
Of that dear city
Pray for me
On the harbour wall
Looking on the spire I'll remember you.

41   Feb 10   Mary & Jesus
Mother running after me
Quickly Mother catch me
I love you so the sun is bright
The day sings joy now find me
Mother here I am run after me.

42   Feb 11   Ancient British Saints 7
Iona beacon in the darkness
Unity with Rome
Her roof above us
The law of Innocents
Light of Columba to lead us home.

34

43   Feb 12   Wisdomword 14

By me kings reign in justice
I love them who love me
Those who seek me find me
Riches and honor I give you
Prosperity that endures.

Mary for peace with Islam! الله

44   Feb 13   柿   Sharon Fruit

Astringent in the memory
Sky opens I see You
How much do I owe Thee
Paul-Fruit I'd name you new
On the tree I am bright & sweet.

45   Feb 14   Sainte Thérèse 8

Listen my little Queen, your patron saint
He was talking about Saint Teresa
I would listen, but my eyes returned to him
I could read so much in his noble face
Sometimes his eyes would fill with tears.

46   Feb 15   Mariazell Basilica 1
With your eye
Follow the tower upwards
On either side stand guardian
Through the gothic portal
Enter my lovely house.

47   Feb 16   Word Flower 5
Sounds like a swift descent
Looks like an icon
Tenderly
Mary loves Jesus
My good mother loves me.

48   Feb 17   Ancient British Saints 8
Take your shoes off and feel the sand
Refresh your soles
Sassenach
We were here first
We're still here & we love, come home.

36

49   Feb 18   Wisdomword 15

The Lord brought me forth as the first of his works
At the very beginning, when the world came to be
When there were no watery depths, I was given birth
When there were no springs overflowing with water
Before the mountains were settled in place.

Mary for peace with Islam! الله

50   Feb 19   Two Sisters

Ma mère régarde à la rivière
La lumière en bleu de ciel
La vie est parabole, the younger I
Flowers and fruits of Eden
Now in red a queen I am in heaven.

51   Feb 20   Sainte Thérèse 9

On my way home I would gaze at the stars
Orion's Belt hung like a string of pearls
I could find the letter T
Look father, I said
My name is written in heaven.

52 Feb 21 Mariazell Basilica 2
Father wore blue sky and sun
A young man carried mother
The joyful choir sang Heilig
People thronged
Hand upon my head he blesses me.

53 Feb 22 Holy Trinity Icon
There are three angels at the table
Their heads gently incline
They listen to thy prayer
In the glass shielding the icon
Look how the candle flames dance.

54 Feb 23 Ancient British Saints 9
King Oswald called me from Iona
Lindisfarne I built on the northern sea
A holy island a platform of the sky
I walked Northumbria
Christ-minded & gifted I gave them Christ.

55 Feb 24 Wisdomword 16

I was there when he set the heavens in place
When he drew a circle on the face of the deep
When he established the clouds above
When he gave the sea its boundary
When he marked out the foundations of the earth.

Mary for peace with Islam! الله

56 Feb 25 Christ Appearing

Young boy kneeling in the highlands
Christ in the mandorla
Gentle father gentle brother
A red tunic and white robe
Shining in the night sky among the stars.

57 Feb 26 Sainte Thérèse 10

That same evening as the sun set
I went with you to sit on a rock
You said it was a path to heaven
My heart I thought was a small ship
With white sails gliding on the path of gold.

58   Feb 27   Joachim & Anna
Before Jerusalem the Golden Gate
Anna clasps his head
Eye & mouth a line together
Holy embrace the haloes melt
Angels rejoice for Mary and her Son.

59   Feb 28   Akashi
Spirit on the waters in the early morning
The boats returning from the night
There you are standing
By the harbor I am waiting for you
Holy Mother bless me and bless my home.

60   Feb 29   Ancient British Saints 10
Monks on a raft swept down the Tyne
Prayed for a wind they were safe
A stream of light & a globe of fire
A great soul went up to heaven
Incorrupt I served and fragrant remain.

61 March 1 Wisdomword 17

I was constantly at His side
I was filled with delight day after day
Rejoicing always in His presence
Rejoicing in His whole world
And delighting in mankind.

Mary for peace with Islam! الله

62 March 2 Mother of God Enthroned

The anointed king was forced to leave
The Blessed Mother in a dream
Led her poor handmaid
They find the long-forgotten icon
My Russian children I am your Queen.

63 March 3 Sainte Thérèse 11

Riven with trauma and suffering
I failed to recognize Marie
My sisters gathered and prayed
A mother's fervor for her own child
Suddenly the statue of Mary came to life.

64   March 4   Postage Stamp

Infant Jesus turning
Wide-eyed to his left
His arms make a letter
Gazing with veiled lids
Mary appears serenely.

65   March 5   Flower in Season

It was a sunny day
Who is the daughter
Giving the Mother a flower
How happy she smiles
Joyful the time.

66   March 6   Ancient British Saints 11

Alone on the island of Inner Farne
Seagulls cry upon the wind
The sea sings with me as I pray
In blessed solitude they are here
Hidden in the sunlight and the sea.

42

67   March 7   Wisdomword 18

Blessed are you who keep my ways
Blessed the one who listens to me
Waiting by the posts of my doors
The one who finds me finds life
You will receive favor from the Lord.

Mary for peace with Islam! الله

68   March 8   Pardonne-leur

Born on the altar
Bleed on the rose
Weep for them
Did what was done
Stand with you Jean.

69   March 9   Sainte Thérèse 12

She appeared so lovely, so tender
Her smile took away my pain
Happy I am I thought
Tears flowed down my cheeks
I recognized Marie.

70   March 10   紅椿   Red Camellia
Flower little lily in the garden
Dance tsubaki in the breeze
Sing bright blossom
Blessed Virgin Mary in Heaven
Brave little one she loves thee greatly.

71   March 11   Daffodil 1
My beloved before thee I kneel
I do not dare to say thy name
How good & how constant
You stand in all weathers
Flowers in thee of all blossoms best.

72   March 12   Ancient British Saints 12
A bright angelic light in his face
With such love for God he spoke
Not one could hide their guilt
They freely confessed their wrong
By penance they took away their sins.

44

73   March 13   Wisdomword 19

Wisdom has built her house with seven pillars
She has prepared the feast
She has sent forth her maidens on the heights
Crying to the people
Let those who need understanding come to me.

Mary for peace with Islam! الله

74   March 14   Pontmain Basilica

My spirit was dry like baked earth
The heart was a barren stone
My mind was at the last point
I walked through to a rainbow
I saw water of light in Pontmain.

75   March 15   Sainte Thérèse 13

Marie asked me and I told her
Feelings changed to bitterness
The tender privacy of my vision
How they questioned me   later
Kneeling to Mary happiness returned.

76   March 16   Cycladic
Stand in front of the glass
Beloved assume
Priapic stone
Adam-love-Eve
She faced the sky   *be fertile*.

77   March 17   Daffodil 2
My head on the earth
A magnified ear
Roots crack
The body stretches
Small voices speak how she grows.

78   March 18   Ancient British Saints 13
My holy relics were moved to Durham
As the ages ran they opened the box
My hallowed blood dried in the bone
Vestments and cross, a gospel book
Children learn from me I live and pray.

79   March 19   Wisdomword 20

The fear of the Lord is the beginning of wisdom
Knowledge of the Holy One is understanding
Through wisdom your days will be many
Being wise you are rewarded by God
Do not be a mocker you will suffer alone.

Mary for peace with Islam! الله

80   March 20   山百合   Yamayuri 2

Not a wand but an armful
A cradle of perfume
Turn and say
Who are you
All these flowers for me?

81   March 21   Sainte Thérèse 14

I was preparing for my first communion
To renew ardor and fill my heart with flowers
I made many sacrifices and acts of love
These were transformed into flowers
All the flowers to cradle Jesus in my heart.

82   March 22   Anchor 1
Paying out the anchor chain
Rattling out the locker
A live thing it goes like thunder
50 thousand pounds of steel
He'll bite the sand and we're safe.

83   March 23   Icon S.M. del P.
Mary my Mother
Heart of the people
Heaven is with thee
Hear our prayer
Heal us to God.

84   March 24   Ancient British Saints 14
That it not lead to biffin
We went to Inishbofin
The date of Holy Easter
The matter of the tonsure
Irish father leading English brothers.

85   March 25   Wisdomword 21

A wise daughter makes a glad father
A foolish daughter is a mother's grief
A daughter who gathers in summer is prudent
A daughter who sleeps in harvest brings shame
Blessings are on the head of the righteous.

Mary for peace with Islam! الله

86   March 26   L'Annunciazione

Alarm bells are ringing
Fearful thrill the heart
Why is it me?
What is it he asks of me
Joyful I am loved by God.

87   March 27   Sainte Thérèse 15

In my heart the first kiss of Jesus
I knew that I was loved and I said
I love you and give myself to you
I was a drop of water in the ocean
Jesus alone remained   Master and King.

88   March 28   Anchor 2

The anchor runs through the pawl
The flukes dig in the sand
Taught at the bitter end
The winds blow & tides pull
My bright star & hope will hold us.

89   March 29   Roettgen Pietà

The pain is over
My poor son
How thin you are
I gave thee life
How art thou gone?

90   March 30   Ancient British Saints 15

The young man is singing a hymn
Carving circles swirling unbreaking
Names of the old and the deeper truth
Miracles in our help under the kingdom loss
In the green life of the wood Jesus & Mary walk.

50

91   March 31   Wisdomword 22

Here is a good word   Love covers all offenses
The mouth of the righteous is a fountain of life
The mouth of the righteous brings forth wisdom
The way of the Lord is a stronghold for the good
The righteous will never be removed.

Mary for peace with Islam! الله

92   Good Friday

After the storm on Galilee subsided
In the smoke on the water I saw him
The manner of the cruel death
Think he said reveal not
The shape of the instrument is dark.

93   Easter Day

I will not say what it meant then
It did not stop there
It will not die
It will open heaven
The instrument is filled with light.

94 Easter   Resurrection Icon
Under your feet the broken tomb
The grave cloth laughs aloud
The sun your mandorla
The cross effulgent
Glorious Christ defeating death!

95 April 1   When
I asked the weatherman
Look how the blossom
Spreads from the south
Look how the autumn
Reddens from the north.

96 April 2   Ancient British Saints 16
At the age of sixteen I was taken captive
Transported with others over the water
I was punished for forgetting God
Daily I prayed for forgiveness
I pastured flocks on an Irish hillside.

52

97   April 3   Wisdomword 23

The city prospers when you bless
Your kindness rewards you
Goodness will live
Your fruit is a tree of life
You will flourish like green leaves.

Mary for peace with Islam! الله

98   April 4   Christ Appears

Young boy kneeling in the highlands
Christ in the mandorla
Gentle father gentle brother
White robe & red gabi
Shine in the night sky among the stars.

99   April 5   Sainte Thérèse 16

I would climb up to the tribune and wait
Father would soon come to fetch me
La terre est ton navire et non pas ta demeure
The line of poetry he taught me
As I thought on this my mind strove to infinity.

100   April 6   Orthodox Kenya
The voice rises up to heaven
The warm tone heals my heart
Lord Jesus in the bread uplifted
The Holy Spirit fills my soul
Blessed be God I cry, the Holy Host.

101   April 7   Crab Apple
Can I remember you?
Happy to be home
The car in the drive
Covered in blossom
The crabs I wished to hoard.

102   April 8   Ancient British Saints 17
As I began to pray the world changed
I fled my keepers and found a boat
As I prayed the boat sped onward
Later a captive then again I was free
God made me a British priest for Eire.

54

103   April 9   Wisdomword 24

The righteous are kind to their animals
The speech of the good saves lives
A kind word gives joy
The root of the godly will yield fruit
The house of the righteous stands firm.

Mary for peace with Islam! الله

104   April 10   Boxing

Stand on guard my little one
My girl
I will teach you defence
Watch him
Dance & dodge & land one.

105   April 11   Sainte Thérèse 17

A picture of the crucifixion slipped out
I saw the wound in his hand
My heart thrilled with sorrow
His precious blood   I decided then
To gather this dew of heaven for others.

106   April 12   連翹   Rengyō

Pure childhood yellow
Arms wide the blessed
Shall I use the word fōs?
Harvest there's the word
A scythe to gather me in.

107   April 13   Sit & Pray 1

Why do you sit cross-legged
They say to me
Holy Mother
I turn to her
She says sit that way and pray.

108   April 14   Ancient British Saints 18

Clear signs I was given to go back to Eire
Not me dear Lord it was your strength
When I prayed the words aloud
The air rang with holy fire
Heaven shook the kings & they kneeled.

56

109 April 15 Wisdomword 25

A daughter loves her father's discipline

Wisdom is in those who take advice

Give correction if you love your children

The light of the righteous shines bright

The teaching of the wise is a fountain of life.

Mary for peace with Islam! الله

110 April 16 Santa Maria del Popolo

The scallop above the doorway

Set in a classical triangle

Cherubs in outstretched wings

Go round the Madonna and infant

Breathes a new delight for God.

111 April 17 Sainte Thérèse 18

His cry as he died "I thirst" echoed in my soul

My heart was inflamed with love

I longed to satisfy his thirst for souls

To save them from the everlasting flame

He let me know he was pleased I felt this way.

112   April 18   Sister Cook
Sushi board dance to the Lord
Chopper and blender sing
Pots and pans clap your hands
Kettle and cauldron fling
Salad spinner spin to the King!

113   April 19   Sit & Pray 2
Sat upon the air above the flower
Otherworldly
Have you no confidence in God?
If I am good
Pity I will for thy death and passion.

114   April 20   Ancient British Saints 19
Sailed in a curragh the corner of the Bay
Under influence of heaven I went far and wee
Tall tales and happenings and whales and filigree
Holy Mass in the boat when I lifted up the Host
The fish in the water said crumbs for us please.

115   April 21   Wisdomword 26

A wise woman builds her house
Her wise speech protects her
She fears the Lord in her righteous way
Be good and you will find love and loyalty
You are blessed because you give to the poor.

Mary for peace with Islam! الله

116   April 22   Spezzano Albanese

Our Lady give healing by Jesus
The foolish ones who test the vision
Jabbing it with a bramble
Blood spurts
Help us not to harm your gentle gifts!

117   April 23   Sainte Thérèse 19

Our hearts light we followed him
The sparks in our souls
The spiced wine to drink
We forgot the world
Love for heaven always on our lips.

118   April 24   Kurara 1
Pale-yellow bells
A pod of black peas
On narrow leaves
My children grow
In time become beauty.

119   April 25   Sit & Pray 3
Children on our visit today please note
Eternal Love
Whose name we speak or cannot speak
Made all
Angels serene in prayer above the flower.

120   April 26   Ancient British Saints 20
He took you for the Mother Mhuire
There was a goddess behind thee
Bride of Ireland gives your name
The sisters fed perpetual flame
Cathedral a milker rests at your feet.

121   April 27   Wisdomword 27

The prayers of the upright delight the Lord
He loves the one who pursues goodness
A glad heart lights up the face
Better is a little with fear of the Lord
Better than treasure with great trouble in it.

Mary for peace with Islam! الله

122   April 28   Virgin with Milk

The window is the mind
The spoon is the scroll
Her translucent veil
His lace chemise
The Lord's breath.

123   April 29   Sainte Thérèse 20

In the evening Céline & I in the belvedere
We gazed on the deepening azure blue
Grace was poured into our souls
God gives himself in radiant light
Sometimes veiled in symbols and shadows.

124   April 30   Rosary on the Coast
They will be saying the rosary on Iona
Let my spirit Lord become a bird
Fly me in dream to join them
To stand in the House of Prayer
To pray Blessed Mother with Columba.

125   May 1   Flower of the Field
Winning bread, clothing the kids
He's not talking about that
The choice of Mary
Dressed in the finest cloth
The holy life in service to the Lord.

126   May 2   Ancient British Saints 21
Fleeing the wicked King they left the boy
Wailing on a rock
A wolf found and nursed him
Long years later the wolf grown old
Seeking safety laid her head upon his lap.

62

127   May 3   Wisdomword 28

The path of the wise leads upward
A wise daughter delights her father
Light in the eyes rejoices the heart
Good news gives health to the bones
The path of the upright is a level highway.

Mary for peace with Islam! الله

128   May 4   Our Lady of Lebanon

Round we go and round we go
Early in the dawn
Sail the sea the boats
One step at a time
Upward to thee Blessed Mother.

129   May 5   Sainte Thérèse 21

Switzerland! Towering mountains
Snow-capped peaks, waterfalls and valleys
Nature did so much good to my soul
God poured His love on this world of exile
It was a taste of Heaven's wonders.

130   May 6   British Woodsman
I squeeze through the narrow trail
Disturb no twig I place my hand
Crouching I move forward
The song of the nightingale loud
I breathe the green and musty earth.

131   May 7   Saint Xenia of Kalamata
Appeared as I prayed a blond angel
My name is Xenia the Martyr
Paint my icon
I will pray for you and family
We found an ancient record of her life.

132   May 8   Ancient British Saints 22
Cross of the Scriptures to teach me
Lifting up a circle to the height
Within the round
The perfect man
Let the cross stand & bless the nation.

133   May 9   Wisdomword 29

A wise son delights his father
Foolish Adam despises his mother
Joyful the daughter who speaks well
How good her word at the right time
Pleasant to the Lord is her pure word.

الله , Mary for peace with Islam!

134   May 10   Wheatgrass

A blue plate of light-brown wheat
Watered & drained in ten days growth
A pale-green stand of tender grass
With my scissors I harvest it
Health I say and drink the juice.

135   May 11   Sainte Thérèse 22

Loreto! This House sheltered the Holy Family
Our Lord looked on these walls
Mary had borne Jesus and held him in her arms
Joseph had worked here. I was deeply moved
My rosary I placed in the bowl Jesus used.

136   May 12   Where's This 25
Saint Mary in Assumption
The Holy Virgin with golden domes
Early Mass hailed a cab
Stood with angels
Strolled down the boulevard to evensong.

137   May 13   Our Lady of Altötting
A gold cape with a red velvet table
Anemones jewels blessed petals
Her hand is a flower
Her scepter is a flower
Her son the flower of flowers best.

138   May 14   Ancient British Saints 23
Oats seethed in warm milk
Written by God on the smooth
The Dun Cow
Moos
Her Latin will not cease.

139   May 15   Wisdomword 30

Humility goes before honor
Learn a good word
Ănāvāh tapeinós humilitas
By humility and fear of the Lord
Granted are riches and honor and life.

Mary for peace with Islam! الله

140   May 16   Coaster

Messages found in curious places
Four queen bees dance in a round
A flower speaks from the heart
Aquamarine in shining silk
Graphs & glyphics secret to Mary.

141   May 17   Sainte Thérèse 23

With special permission the priest said Mass
We were in the Santa Casa within the Basilica
That communion was a joy beyond words
We became His living temple, Jesus in our hearts
Alive in the very House in which he dwelt on earth.

142   May 18   Valaam Icon 1
My old body racked with pain
I threw myself on the mercy of Our Mother
Within my heart a voice said *Go to Valaam*
In complete destitution I went
Mother to my prayer you came and healed me.

143   May 19   Myrrh 1
Murmur to thee my little boy
Fragrant white flowers in spring
The milky resin hardens in the air
Mummy you will say to me tomorrow
The gift will serve us in the time to come.

144   May 20   Ancient British Saints 24
I remember Ireland
The soft rain falling on the grey stone
The grass never stopped growing
Green for the love of it
Sweet water we prayed there.

145   May 21   Wisdomword 31

Commit to the Lord
He will establish your hope
The lot is cast in the lap
Only the Lord will decide it
Plans are mortal, God gives the answer.

Mary for peace with Islam! الله

146   May 22   Our Lady of Help 1

A blazon of golden rays behind her
Our Lady walks from the house
Look! Her infant is a king
She holds a scepter in her hand
Glorious she is the Queen of Heaven.

147   May 23   Sainte Thérèse 24

Speak whispered Céline. I knelt before him
He gave me his hand. I raised my eyes
Most Holy Father I want to ask a great favor
He bent his head down almost touching mine
His piercing black eyes gazed into my soul.

148   May 24   Our Lady of Help 2

Praying on my knees in the pew
Guide me my Mother
Here I am child
You lift up Jesus to me
Auxiliadora with beautiful hair.

149   May 25   Bede's Prayer

O Christ, our Morning Star
Splendor of Light Eternal
Shining with the glory of the rainbow
Come and waken us from accidie
Renew in us your gift of hope, Amen.

150   May 26   Ancient British Saints 25

Lessons to survival how he gave
The good of the house to the poor
And still gave beyond all sense
And built us a poem-place
A craft-house a wisdom-ship to sail.

70

151   May 27   Wisdomword 32

When a king's face brightens
It means life
His favor is like a rain cloud in spring
Gracious words are a honeycomb
Sweet to the soul and healing to the bones.

Mary for peace with Islam! الله

152   May 28   Sacra Famiglia

Dancing on her hands
Running out to you
Father I am mindful of you
Father your love pours down
Mother I'm holding your robe & my word.

153   May 29   Sainte Thérèse 25

O Très Saint Père, si vous disiez oui
Tout le monde voudrait bien
Allons   Allons   si le bon Dieu le veut
If you said yes everyone would agree
Well then   if the Good Lord wants it to happen.

154   May 30   Rest on the Flight to Egypt

We are resting by the cool rocks
The donkey found some grazing
Joseph gathers providential fruit
Mary is feeding me and I
Well I am happy at the source.

155   May 31   Valaam Icon 2

O suffering mother little Russian saint
How your story moves me
Pray for me моя милая мать
Help me Christ to find your Mother
Within my world   my life   my soul!

156   June 1   Ancient British Saints 26

Still holding out your stiff arm
The body gone to atoms
Specks are alive
Floating on the breeze
Seeding the stream to me here.

72

157   June 2   Wisdomword 33

A friend loves at all times
A brother is born to help in trouble
A cheerful heart is good medicine
The words of the mouth are deep waters
There is a friend more loyal than a brother.

Mary for peace with Islam! الله

158   June 3   Valaam Icon 3

In red imperial gown
Holy Mother of God
Standing on a cloud
In bright gold set
Hold up thy son to us.

159   June 4   Sainte Thérèse 26

Sainte Madeleine de Pazzi in Florence
We all wanted to place our rosaries
On her tomb behind the grate
Only my hand was small enough
Her blessing on our prayer.

160 June 5 Igorevskaya Icon
Mother look from heaven
Holy prince Igor
Soul arises
Your son embraces
Saint Igor is blest with God.

161 June 6 Krakowiak 2
Ponies prancing round we go
Yearlings leaping
Lads and maidens standing
Singing
Joy to me the dance is bringing!

162 June 7 Ancient British Saints 27
Patient in stillness breathing
I will wait like Kevin in the cold
Calling to thee Mother Mary
To my finger tip send your angel
Thy bright Chickadee.

74

163   June 8   Wisdomword 34

The name of the Lord is a strong tower
The righteous run to it and are safe
A discerning mind acquires knowledge
Wise ears are always ready to learn
A gift opens doors, to petition the great.

Mary for peace with Islam! الله

164   June 9   Water Shrew

In the water again before you blink
A trail of bubbles breaks above
I sing a shrill song
Happy when I smell a worm
Praying when the mink is in the air.

165   June 10   Sainte Thérèse 27

From Florence to Pisa to Genoa
The railway ran beside the sea for miles
The waves seemed to wash our wheels
Then through orange groves, olives and palms
In the evening the seaports were ablaze with lights.

166   June 11   Dance for Mary 1

Performing the sword dance
I flicker my heels for thee
In the skirling wailing
Not touching the blades
I'll sing thy name as I dance.

167   June 12   Mother Icon

From the gown her pearly arm
Reaches to embrace him
Holding his head
Joyful he's laughing
Mother you sing me an old song.

168   June 13   Ancient British Saints 28

Pray for me Saint Kevin
The wolf in me be tame
The blackbird in me sing
The otter in me swim to thee
Mirror of Glendalough show heaven

76

169   June 14   Wisdomword 35

When you are good to the poor
You lend to the Lord. He will repay you
It is good sense to be slow to anger
It is glory to ignore a wrong
Obtain wisdom and love your true self.

Mary for peace with Islam! الله

170   June 15   青花   Aobana

The morning dew
Poured the sky
On my square
Staining sapphire
An Ave I gave to Maria.

171   June 16   Sainte Thérèse 28

Father was planning a pilgrimage to Jerusalem
To visit the places He hallowed
I was weary of earthly pilgrimages
I longed only for the beauty of heaven
To be a prisoner to win those beauties for others.

172   June 17   Dance for Mary 2
Light upon my toes springing
A deer through the glen
Round I go dancing
North and South
Left & Right I leap & I prance.

173   June 18   浦島草   Urashimasō 1
Corona a wreath of golden-green
Mottled purple and white
My true glory
In the early morning I sing
A long line of perfect song to God.

174   June 19   Ancient British Saints 29
Fame of the Irish in the world
Passion for the Christ
In the ruins of the castle
School of love for God
Perfect Gospel all things common.

175   June 20   Wisdomword 36

The Lord gives light to the human spirit

He searches out our inmost heart

He brings us to his light

The righteous walk in integrity

Happy are the children who follow Him.

Mary for peace with Islam! الله

176   June 21   Book of Kells 1

Lapis Lazuli blue and indigo

The parchment is calf

A holy bird

A rainbow harp

Singing I come from Heaven.

177   June 22   Sainte Thérèse 29

My dream of life in the Carmel!

At last peace filled my soul

My little cell delighted me

The path was thorns & roses

The daily bread at first was hard.

178   June 23   Dance for Mary 3
In the air I float for thee
No life without thee
If you dance not with me
How can I dance
Dance with me darling!

179   June 24   Kurara 2
Sapphire wings with splotches
Edges dark-brown to black
The tail orange-brown
Banded antenna
Beautiful eye.

180   June 25   Ancient British Saints 30
Where fair he taught let love be shown
Learning he had and saintly life
On holy isle Guagán Barra
He prayed for Cork and all her kin
He lives in two great houses powerful saint.

80

181   June 26   Wisdomword 37

A good name is better than wealth

To be esteemed is better than gold

The generous will be blessed

They share their food with the poor

Humility is rewarded with riches and long life.

Mary for peace with Islam! الله

182   June 27   Book of Kells 2

Witness to the Irish we live

In the swirling unfinished

Salvation of Jesus Christ

Saxon Viking & Pict

God and His mother are Celt!

183   June 28   Sainte Thérèse 30

The cross the way to win souls

To save souls and pray for priests

This was the hidden flower for Jesus

This was the perfume to rise to heaven

Each sacrifice I could offer to Him.

184   June 29   Passion Flower 1
I turned to the flower
The long and short arm
How much time remains
It has gone inside out
Galactic blossom.

185   June 30   Rose en Sucre
Watch the clever fingers
Quick as quick they go
Kneading and forming
Of a sudden look!
It is a golden rose.

186   July 1   Ancient British Saints 31
Open the fush said Mungo
A golden ring in the salmon's beak
Cover a sin and save a marriage
Forgive one another and carry on
Who says that saints do not teach truth?

187 July 2 Wisdomword 38

Apply your mind to instruction
Your ear to words of knowledge
My child, if your heart is wise
If your lips speak what is right
Your mother will rejoice in heart & soul.

Mary for peace with Islam! الله

188 July 3 Book of Kells 3

Saints on the edge of the world
Far from authority
Book of Kells you teach me
What we should do
Embellish our love with our life.

189 July 4 Sainte Thérèse 31

The treasures of his face
You taught me to find them
I understood the mysteries
His kingdom is not of this world
True royalty is known by being humble.

190   July 5   Passion Flower 2
I turned to the flower
She turned to me
Just past half past
The afternoon sun
Moved shadow on wall.

191   July 6   上海飴細工   Shanghai Amezaiku
A pan of brown sugar
A white marble board
A large spoon he drew
A dancing curving
Glorious line a joyful dragon.

192   July 7   Ancient British Saints 32
Son of a prince gifted in speech
Liquid brook running Welsh
Delightful in synod
His governance leading
Founding the Church Llan Dewi.

193   July 8   Wisdomword 39

The vineyard was overgrown with thorns
Thick with nettles, the wall was broken
A little sleep, a little quiet rest, and lo!
Like an armed man or a robber
Poverty stands at your door.

Mary for peace with Islam! الله

194   July 9   Marinera Nortena 1

Look how they dance upon the breeze
Her skirts lifted up like wings
He dances the soul's joy
When she found the beloved
Close they almost kiss and lightly dance.

195   July 10   Sainte Thérèse 32

He found a way of shaking hands
He spoke so kindly
He took a holy delight
It seemed he had not noticed
Or maybe had forgotten the insult.

196   July 11   Passion Flower 3

So let it flower

Eye close to fibre

Scratching out letters

Snuffing up papyrus

Unrolling song.

197   July 12   Mother Sculpture

We made bricks from the earth

It's not an arch, you know

Two angels put their heads together

Maybe it's a misnomer

The wind sings through a gap.

198   July 13   Ancient British Saints 33

Not a story to make you laugh

Daughter of a king

Wickedly possessed

He chased, she fled, said no

The end. Yet her goodness doth heal.

199   July 14   Wisdomword 40

If your enemies hunger, give them bread

If they thirst, give them water

Subdue the will to revenge

Silence the voice of anger

How greatly the Lord God will reward you.

Mary for peace with Islam! الله

200   July 15   Marinera Nortena 2

Beautiful the feet upon the mountains

Wings of the white birds on sea

In my hand the sunshine

Out of the sky I am dancing

Earth and sky Mary my bride for thee.

201   July 16   Sainte Thérèse 33

A bridal gown with diamonds and jewels

Beautiful enough to be your bride

How could I reach perfection

I thought what else is there to learn

The more I advance the further off it seems.

202   July 17   Fairy Reel
Heels and toes before and after
The lines weave in and out
Hands change hands
Returning laughter
Reels round and round about.

203   July 18   Snowy Egret
Walking in the uplands
A soft undulation
The ground carrying water
Day of sun in monsoon
There she stood like a white bird.

204   July 19   Ancient British Saints 34
Margaret mother of Henry built thee
How deeply you were loved
And what well-springs of faith
To the gates of the present day
You lived, and now you grow.

205   July 20   Wisdomword 41
Do not boast about tomorrow
You do not know what a day may bring
Let another praise you and not yourself
As face mirrors face in the water
So one heart reflects another.

Mary for peace with Islam! الله

206   July 21   Inca Dance
Under the white
Through the cloud
Into the blue
Above the white mist soar
Clear bright air condor wings.

207   July 22   Sainte Thérèse 34
Desperate   to know my vocation false
To the Novice Mistress
I must leave
No, she said, all is good
My humility brought surpassing peace.

208   July 23   Puhtitsa
A summer day procession
Flowers where the family sleep
Gospod Pomolimsa thrum
Christos Bog on high
In the sky I find the Holy Mother.

209   July 24   DC-3 Design 1
Cut the aesthetics free
The beauty of the design
With arms held wide
We climb from a grassy field
Argentina   look!   the Andes.

210   July 25   Ancient British Saints 35
In the Idylls I crowned the king
A fictional truth
In my prayer I crown him always
Christ in sanctity and strength
I taught the youth to be holy.

211 July 26 Wisdomword 42

Do not bless a friend with a loud voice early
As iron sharpens iron
So one may sharpen another
She who tends the fig tree may eat its fruit
She who cares for her master will be honored.

Mary for peace with Islam! ﷲ

212 July 27 Saint Alphonsa

Powerful healer
Seize my feet
With holy hands
Pulling & pushing
Help me to walk.

213 July 28 Sainte Thérèse 35

I pronounced my sacred vows
I laid my crown of roses
At Our Lady's feet
The Nativity of Mary
Our Lady gave her little flower.

214   July 29   Feria de las Flores
She strapped on the silleta
Brown pillar hat
A schoolroom of kinder
Bare feet whacked the tarmac
Singing she heaves them up to Mary.

215   July 30   DC-3 Design 2
He never intended you for that
We are born from you
You carried us
Your arms stretch wide
Your face is a dove or a flower.

216   July 31   Ancient British Saints 36
Find me in the ancient name
Holy vessels keep the honey
I taught the Breton mission
Mary the Blessed Mother
Held us safely in her hands.

92

217   Aug 1   Wisdomword 43

The wise quietly restrain anger
She who trusts in the Lord is secure
She who is lowly in spirit obtains honor
She who loves wisdom brings joy to her father
You are blessed if you listen to wisdom's instruction.

Mary for peace with Islam!   الله

218   Aug 2   Irish Stamp

A word from Clare
Under green water
Firework flower
My thoughts ignite
Sky blossoms in light.

219   Aug 3   Sainte Thérèse 36

The story of the little flower
God's mercy with her always
I bless the Mother who gave me to Jesus
I will be a flower in your crown
I will sing the canticle of love that is ever new.

93

220   Aug 4   提灯   Chōchin
They were carrying paper lanterns
Bright candles within
White globes with red rings
Within the tondo the face of a saint
Mother Mary look Saint Francis Xavier.

221   Aug 5   Mary Dancing
Dance my daughters
Round in a circle
The hills are dancing
Dance on the water
The love of God.

222   Aug 6   Ancient British Saints 37
My relics divided miraculously in three
Saints live and die and words fade
In place names we live on
They will tell stories & I tell truth
Christ Jesus is the doorway to our God.

94

223 Aug 7 Wisdomword 44

Who has gone up to heaven and come down again
Who has cupped the wind in the hollow of the hand
Who has bound up the waters in a cloak
Who has established all the ends of the earth
What is that person's name, or the name of his son?

Mary for peace with Islam! ﷲ

224 Aug 8 Querrien

In the water of the holy spring there it is
An ancient statue of mother & infant
In this place I shall be honored
Our Lady of Help who heals
To the pardon the Breton pilgrims come.

225 Aug 9 Lily

Bronze pillars with lilies
Stand and sing
Lift your calyx
Honey of the throat
Flower in the house of God.

226   Aug 10   Br. Junipero
Kneel by her picture
Light a candle for Saint Clare
Brother Junipero lend a hand
Fire my prayer with fervent hope
Saint Clare in heaven pray for us, amen.

227   Aug 11   Clare Procession
The brass band blares a joyful blast
The people cheer
On our shoulders she walks
Holy Host of Christ her hand upholds
Our fingers hold the grill we bless the town.

228   Aug 12   Ancient British Saints 38
2000 years on my back
Looking for the sources
When we were children
The pool was fed by a spring
Pray with me first Christians.

229   Aug 13   Wisdomword 45

The tiny ant gathers her food in the summer
The humble hyrax builds a house in the rock
The locusts sally forth in mighty formation
The lowly lizard lives in the king's palace
The smallest creatures show God's wisdom.

Mary for peace with Islam!   الله

230   Aug 14   Walsingham Well

Water from the well drink with my blessing
The saints walked in this land
Family we prayed together
In hardship, in sorrow, in joy
Healing water by thy Mother Lord *she lives!*

231   Aug 15   Assumption

Twelve apostles stand amazed
Marble vault filled with lilies
Above their heads
The sky is ranked with angels
The Blessed Virgin is the Queen.

232   Aug 16   Mari Txindoli
Mother of the Vascones
Should not our Mother dwell on high
From the first the seat of holiness
Montserrat   Montblanc   Jungfrau
Her name the same because

233   Aug 17   多羅葉   Tarayō
Broad lustrous oval leaves
Turn to the pale side
Write a poem
Wait until it appears
Send it to the one you love.

234   Aug 18   Ancient British Saints 39
The Lord in the saints shouts
Flee to the setting sun
We stood behind the Tamar
A saint in every village
Christ held them and we lived.

235   Aug 19   Wisdomword 46

Can you find a word of wisdom here
The proud and mighty lion
He will not give way to anyone
The strutting rooster, the billy-goat
The king who strides before his army.

Mary for peace with Islam! الله

236   Aug 20   Lithops

I was outside the walls
Sitting on a rock
Not far from Gihon spring
A man from Bethany on a donkey
Under the olives the stones began to sing.

237   Aug 21   Little Way 1

I will find a little way to heaven
Very short and direct
We live in an age of inventions
An elevator will take me straight to Jesus
The steep stairway is too hard for me.

238   Aug 22   Carob

In the shade of the grateful tree
His limbs spare as the fruit
His face burnt black
His backbone gnarled
His head the tree bright in sun.

239   Aug 23   Clareclown

Red stripy vest and giant shoes
I'm chasing out the blues
Waking up the grans
Vespers I'm in brown
Salve Regina I'm walking in a line.

240   Aug 24   Ancient British Saints 40

In the darkness of the coal-black night
    They fill the wicker baskets
      Shines an alabaster cross
        Two streams of light
Shine until the world itself shall end.

241 Aug 25 Wisdomword 47

Who can find a virtuous woman?
Her price is far above rubies
The heart of her husband doth trust in her
He will be satisfied with her goodness
He shall have no need of spoil.

Mary for peace with Islam! الله

242 Aug 26 Embroider

Blessed Virgin Holy Theotokos
Singing Ave Maria
With my fingers
I write lines of thread
A thousand prayers by thy grace.

243 August 27 Little Way 2

I searched the Scriptures for a hint
Words of eternal wisdom
Whosoever is little let them come to me
As a mother caresses her infant
I will carry and comfort you.

244   Aug 28   Kurara 3
Whispers a cold wind
Thy saints are false
Thy gift worthless
Thy hope gone
On the air I'll float and win.

245   Aug 29   Resolute
Jesus set his face toward Jerusalem
We live in a community of sisters
Our lives spent together close as family
One has gone into care, O the loss of her
Praying for her resolutely we go onward.

246   Aug 30   Ancient British Saints 41
Padstow from Petrocstow
Names are all we have and stories
Water when I struck the Cornish rock
Bodmin holy relics were stolen by a thief
Ivory casket   *Family I lived! We are alive in heaven.*

247 Aug 31 Wisdomword 48

She does him good
All the days of her life
She seeks wool and flax
She works with willing hands
She weaves the cloth with delight.

Mary for peace with Islam! الله

248 Sept 1 Festa della Rificolona

In honor of our Mother's birth
We process in a joyful crowd
Our lanterns swing
A lion-face, a friendly wolf
We fling them in the happy flame.

249 Sept 2 Little Way 3

Preferring this and disliking that
Our natural feelings are wrong
Her discourteous manner
A sister who annoys with every word
Can you be patient yet and love and love?

250   Sept 3   Teresa Film
Almost fifty years since that famous film
Mother Teresa revealed to the world
The Calcutta sunlight on her sari
The new Mary Sisters visit the elderly
The headlines run, Japan! Angel in Kimono.

251   Sept 4   St Rose of Viterbo
On fire for God in the first word she spoke
Miracles at her hands through her life
Her mother's sister she raised
Too poor to be admitted to the Clares
Receive my body after my death, she said.

252   Sept 5   Ancient British Saints 42
Where your tomb is found
A well of water
Your holy chair
Three seats in arches
Above the central arch a crown.

253 Sept 6 Wisdomword 49

The merchant galley on the seas
She brings her gifts from afar
She rises in the night-time
She prepares the family food
She gives one part to her maidens.

Mary for peace with Islam! الله

254 Sept 7 Our Lady of Mantara

We sealed up the entrance with rocks
We left our homes and hid in the hills
Generations lived and died
Our glory did not fade
Our love of God & His Blessed Mother.

255 Sept 8 Little Way 4

We were washing clothes in the laundry
Sister splashing me with dirty water
How I wanted to say something
I smiled and bore it patiently
Half an hour to enjoy this new aspersion.

256   Sept 9   Zampoña
Breathe a soft & rapid note
Mary the melody run round
Before I think I move
Within thy song I dance
Mother I am happy with thee.

257   Sept 10   Cirrocumulus
Majesty slept in the hills
Awaken
He flew on the water
Spread through the sky
Shone like a candle flame.

258   Sept 11   Ancient British Saints 43
From Ireland with companions
Fleeing persecution
Said to be a midwife
Frescoes on my walls
I was a holy sister choosing God.

259   Sept 12   Wisdomword 50

She chooses a field and buys it
With the money she made
She plants a vineyard
She girds herself with strength
Her arms are mighty in her work.

Mary for peace with Islam! الله

260   Sept 13   Kurara 4

The larvae build the house
They sleep in the earth
They rise with May wings
They delight the world
On a warm wind they came.

261   Sept 14   Little Way 5

I want Jesus to draw me into the flames of His love
To live and act within me at one with Himself
The more the fire of love inflames my heart
The more I shall say draw me
The more I will run in the sweet odor of the Beloved.

262   Sept 15   Akita Harvest
Riding the wind over Akita
Skimming the harvest
Heads turning yellow
The sunlight warm
The breeze waves through.

263   Sept 16   Palmyra
Chop away the outer
Pulpy black-purple
The inner that I want
Sweet translucent gel
In a tall glass with ice.

264   Sept 17   Ancient British Saints 44
Sing out the names rejoicing
Saint Just Saint Mawes Saint Austell
Saint Buryan pray for us
Saint Cury pray for us
God bless Kernow & all her folk, amen.

265   Sept 18   Wisdomword 51

Her work profits the house
Her lamp does not go out
It burns through the night
Her hands upon the distaff
Her fingers work the spindle.

                                                                     Mary for peace with Islam! ﷲ

266   Sept 19   Jakarta Dances

Little flowers dance for Paul
Petal hands and petal feet
The wooden xylophones
Ring out the beat
Dance with joy in Jesus Christ.

267   Sept 20   Little Way 6

Mother Anne of Jesus who founded Carmel
Tell me Mother   does God want more of me
My little way the things I do for Him
God is pleased with you, she said
The warmth of the dream is with me still.

268   Sept 21   Hulling Rice
Mother is wearing a red sari
Rice swept in the hollow
Treading the huller
Lifts the arm up
Thud! The iron strikes the rice.

269   Sept 22   Villager Dances
Saint Paul sister standing close
The brother dances
An ancient tale
Feathers on his head
Honor thee beloved with my love.

270   Sept 23   Ancient British Saints 45
Britons to the Bretons
Boats with Irish cousins
A Celtic cross to stand outside
Weathered stone wears feathery cloth
Family is a saint we must remember them.

271   Sept 24   Wisdomword 52

She reaches out to the poor
Her hands to help them
Her strength to the needy
She has little fear of snow
The household is warmly dressed.

Mary for peace with Islam! الله

272   Sept 25   Alexandrian Muscat

Cool breeze in the vineyard at seven
The sunlight upon the muscat
The globes glowing
Africa before me as I pray
Standing in the hills looking south.

273   Sept 26   Little Way 7

I will show you yet a better way

Jesus, I have found my true vocation
Summed up in love and love is all
Love will give life to the mystical body
In the heart of Mother Church I will be love.

274   Sept 27   Yam
Read it backwards
God fruited the earth
We were lowest and poorest
We stand up strong
Mary yam.

275   Sept 28   Novitiate Dances
Four sisters in the sunshine
Bright clouds above
Golden sarongs
One length of cloth
Hands holding dance for Jesus.

276   Sept 29   Ancient British Saints 46
One of the seven Breton saints
From Gwent I come on fire with Christ
A servant of God in Saint-Servan
I found the church which bears my name
On the long sands I walk and pray.

277 Wisdomword 53

Her clothing is fine linen and purple
She makes good linen garments
The household is dressed in crimson
Her husband is known in the gates
He sits among the elders of the land.

Mary for peace with Islam! الله

278 Oct 1 Solemn Profession

They plant a Madonna on Carmel
Fragrant Lilium candidum
Sun stays upon the white petal
Sun-yellow in the heart
Lily you renew me you give me life.

279 Oct 2 Meaning of Icons 23

Theology and iconography
The insoluble problem
To express by ways
Belonging to creation
The infinitely higher truth.

280   Oct 3   Earth Fruits
Knobbly eyed indomitable
Cobbles on the stand
Orange & white in halves
Purple & mauve
Sweetly my God you bless me.

281   Oct 4   Hādār   Citron
Teachers explain
Hadar like hadir a sheep-pen
Hadar like hydor water
Hadar is beauty the only
From Moses' time we knew.

282   Oct 5   Ancient British Saints 47
A pilgrim on the Tro Breizh
In Vannes I stand before the altar
The Holy Blessed Virgin stand above
Lift up the banners high
Bishop Patern in purple & gold proceed!

283 Oct 6 Wisdomword 54

Strength and dignity are her clothing
She laughs at the time to come
She opens her mouth with wisdom
Kindness is on her tongue
She defends with the bread of hard work.

Mary for peace with Islam! الله

284 Oct 7 Our Lady of Good Help 1

Vision in my life
Mary the Holy Mother to me
Teach the young and guide them
Give knowledge of the sacraments
The sign of the Cross. I will help you.

285 Oct 8 Meaning of Icons 24

As we stand before the iconostasis
The voice of the holy teacher
Look on Jesus & His Mother
Learn the twelve holy days
The Prophets, the Fathers & Angels.

286   Oct 9   Our Lady
To and fro the rally goes
Our Lady thru
The trees singing
Lightly dance
On the fields of harvest.

287   Oct 10   Our Lady of Good Help 2
There was no money
We lived through lean years
Praying to the Blessed Virgin
Our Lady speak to Jesus
Send us some bread.

288   Oct 11   Ancient British Saints 48
With my psalter honed sharp
I would take a slice of fish
From a prayerful carp
With everlasting flesh
In my house my statue you may find.

289   Oct 12   Wisdomword 55

Praise her for the work of her hands
    Her children
        Her husband
            Her house
Let her praise ring out in the gates of heaven.

Mary for peace with Islam! الله

290   Oct 13   Our Lady of Good Help 3

Mary pioneered in Wisconsin
Lumber good and the grass rich
My father built the chapel
By wagon & locomotive
Belgium came to the new land.

291   Oct 14   Meaning of Icons 25

Raise your eyes to the Deisis
In Slav this is called the Tchin
Christ in glory sits on his throne
In rhythmic perfection they stand
Undying voices of eternal prayer.

292   Oct 15   Walk to Mary 1
I closed my eyes
Pilgrims were talking
I could see a great river
Mississippi   grand Missouri
Bright water of the Colorado.

293   Oct 16   Walk to Mary 2
From St Joseph in Green Bay
Tell me then how has she changed you
I do what I never did before I care for people
Ask him   they came from Belgium
150 years & we're still here   still walking.

294   Oct 17   Ancient British Saints 49
From the British to the Bretons
To teach the Holy Gospel
In a small boat I sail
Warm currents
On yellow sands come dancing.

295   Oct 18   Wisdomword 56

Honor your mother as long as she lives
Do not grieve her in any way
Make her heart rejoice
She carried you in her womb
Remember how much trouble she bore.

Mary for peace with Islam! الله

296   Oct 19   St Peter of Alcantara

An hour or two of sleep per day
Days went by he never ate
His body was a shriveled tree
Forward, he said, in good reform
The root drink God & Church renew.

297   Oct 20   Meaning of Icons 26

The image and the likeness of God
Perfect man is restored in him
Two natures united in one
The falling of the son of Man
The exaltation of the son of God.

298   Oct 21   Where's this? 26
Standing beneath a coconut tree
A tree of life
Saint Christopher carries Jesus
His head bowed
The steadfast Filipino bears up God.

299   Oct 22   Nyiur
Bless thy head
Wave-rider
White-lined
Hairy urn
Go peaceful shores.

300   Oct 23   Ancient British Saints 50
The name Léon may derive from legion
In my legend I subdued a dragon
What should that be
But the Saxon
In my great house stand with me in light.

301   Oct 24   Wisdomword 57

Give charity my child
Out of wealth give abundantly
From little give what you can
Do not hesitate to give charity
It is treasure stored against adversity.

Mary for peace with Islam! الله

302   Oct 25   Eel

Bury my head
I will arise
From the sky
Eat my flesh
Drink my milk.

303   Oct 26   Meaning of Icons 27

Mandorla   the Icon of the Sign
Shall I reveal the significance
Isaiah speaks
A virgin shall conceive
Behold Immanuel in her womb.

304   Oct 27   Duke Humfrey
Flowering window
Shall I climb your rungs
Let the light upon you
Be the morning of my life
A book to honor Mary the rose.

305   Oct 28   Name Again 14
Do not go to their cities
They went to their village
He saw him and felt pity
Why do you ask me for water
They believed because of her.

306   Oct 29   Ancient British Saints 51
A monk from Wales
Mission for Christ
I found a monastery
My fountain flows
By my bones you may pray.

307 Oct 30 Wisdomword 58

Do to no one what you yourself hate
Discipline yourself in all conduct
Do not drink wine to excess
Give food to the hungry
Give clothing to the naked.

Mary for peace with Islam! الله

308 Oct 31 大根 Daikon

To the blue height there is no cloud
I hang my verse to the Amur wind
Parching shrinking
Sweetens
Mother's milk.

309 Nov 1 Meaning of Icons 28

Hodigitria   She who guides
Majestic she stares to the right
Full-face he looks upon us
He gives his benediction
The Mother shows the Son.

310   Nov 2   Oils
Camphor to soothe and loosen
Pine to clear the head
Olive in my lamps
Frankincense I pray
Myrrh to keep me when I sleep.

311   Nov 3   Name Again 15
Mary dances with a tambourine
Exult in the victory of Christ
The monster and his man
Entombed in the sea
Dark waters open & we go free.

312   Nov 4   Ancient British Saints 52
Nephew of Brieuc
To Armorica together
He founds the monastery
And leaves me in charge
Remembering Calvary I walk the cloister.

313   Nov 5   Wisdomword 59

Seek counsel from the wise
At all times bless the Lord your God
Ask him to make your paths straight
May he give good speed to all you do
The Lord himself gives all good things.

_{Mary for peace with Islam!} الله

314   Nov 6   Kalimantan Dance

Little Marys in white
Our love flowers
Kalimantan
Daughters dance
Sisters we dance for God.

315   Nov 7   Meaning of Icons 29

Notice her eyes and long neck
The maphorion with three stars
Perpetual virginity is shown
Christ-child Emmanuel himation
See how it is woven entirely of gold.

316   Nov 8   Zoom Out
The angel took me up
The world, the milky way
Shrank to a dot all shrinking
An ocean of stars to a tiny dewdrop
Still farther then a flowery mead appeared.

317   Nov 9   Name Again 16
From Hebrew we change into Greek
Read me back in Hebrew again
A drop of the sea we sail upon
Now we are Latin   Lord
Thy bright star shine on the scribe!

318   Nov 10   Ancient British Saints 53
Mighty in name long-haired from Wales
Holy prodigy from my youth
The poisonous serpent in his lair
I put to flight and I raised up
A monastery on holy wells.

126

319   Nov 11   Wisdomword 60

Give thanks to God
Give praise and glory
Speak of the good he has done
Bless and extol his name in song
Honor God   do not be slow.

Mary for peace with Islam! الله

320   Nov 12   What's the Saint's Name?

Waiting eagerly for the kingdom of God
Stars of the morning so gloriously bright
Russian Orthodox I give you light
Pity poor children in the Roman street
A gape I am in wonder   O Maria ti vido!

321   Nov 13   Meaning of Icons 30

Can you tell the difference
Her head & body turns to him
His body turns to her
Tenderness and majesty
Look there! What does that mean?

322   Nov 14   Gate Bridge
Lift up your heads
Shout out in joy
Upon the ocean
Thru all the world
Friend! Be welcome in my home.

323   Nov 15   Name Again 17
You take the yoke from my shoulders
You lead me by a cord
A gentle word
I am patient and kind
I care for you with love and feed you.

324   Nov 16   Ancient British Saints 54
Word of their ferocity dismayed me
Encouraged by our father we went on
Their gentleness and the Holy Spirit
In beautiful Latin turns to English
The king received the purity of Christ.

128

325   Nov 17   Wisdomword 61

A king's secret be kept
In a good time speak out
The works of God be revealed
Praise them all with honor
Do good always.

Mary for peace with Islam! الله

326   Nov 18   Palm Oil 1

God's hands gave us the palms
Boil the red fruits until tender
Mash them to a fibrous pulp
Take out kernels & squeeze
Oil between your fingers fill the bowl.

327   Nov 19   Meaning of Icons 31

Hodigitria transformed
Close-up to her shoulders
How tenderly she looks
Contemplation on my son
His passion and his glory.

328   Nov 20   Akashi Bridge
Little one dream
Walk from Kobe
Whirlpools below
Good land before
Go back to the start.

329   Nov 21   Name Again 18
Why do they spell it like
The first will be last he said
Let me just jot this down
Hebrew & Greek & Latin
Well, she has a holy name.

330   Nov 22   Ancient British Saints 55
God mi gard she sang in Frank
Fear of the old gods melted
Might of the Almighty
In the hands of Ethelbert
Built the English with good laws.

331   Nov 23   Wisdomword 62

Raphael said, No need to fear
You are safe
Thank God now and forever
I come to you by the will of God
Praise him with song every day.

Mary for peace with Islam! الله

332   Nov 24   Palm Oil 2

Steel cylinder with eyes
Long spiral screw shaft
We fill it with the mash
We spin the lever round
Lo the oil runs out rich & red.

333   Nov 25   Meaning of Icons 32

The Mother seated in majesty
Her son enthroned on her lap
Michael & Gabriel left & right
Her hand on his left shoulder
His robe or the scroll he holds?

334   Nov 26   Meganebashi
We are bridge builders you and I
Walk with me old chap
Stand here and say
Let the way
Lead us to love one another more.

335   Nov 27   Name Again 19
The name & saw it was good
Appeared white as snow
Transit name ululate
Founded upon the name
Seize the name all praise Him.

336   Nov 28   Ancient British Saints 56
First Christian king
In this fair land
Lord Jesus Christ
Mother Mary's love
Halig Heofones Cyning!

337 Nov 29 Wisdomword 63
Praise the Lord for his goodness
Bless the King of the ages
May his tent be rebuilt in you
A light will shine throughout the earth
Many nations will come to Jerusalem.

Mary for peace with Islam! الله

338 Nov 30 Our Lady of Charity 1
Blessed Virgin Mary on the sea
Floating miraculously
Caridad to Cuba
Come home with me
Bless our people with Charity.

339 Dec 1 Meaning of Icons 33
Mercy herself is transfigured
Tenderly the child and the mother
Pray before the icon to understand
Holy Father this is thy compassion
Fill my heart with love for all creation.

340　　Dec 2　　Kimono
It was the monthly visit
On her own
Lily white kimono
In the hallway
Mother Mary bless this house.

341　　Dec 3　　Name Again 20
母音　Mary help me say
韻母　in a rhyme
声母　on the first day
生母　He created
母性　He gave the way.

342　　Dec 4　　Ancient British Saints 57
Baptized with Edwin by Paulinus
Great gathering at Whitby
In child and mother I live on
My daughters and my sons
You are the Holy English Church.

134

343   Dec 5   Wisdomword 64

What has been is what will be
What has been done is what will be done
There is nothing new under the sun
Is there a thing of which it is said
See, this is new? It has already been.

Mary for peace with Islam! الله

344   Dec 6   Poinsettia

Felt better for you
Ancient crimson
Cloth of glory
Forest-green
Let's wait for spring.

345   Dec 7   Meaning of Icons 34

Vladimir thy holy Russian icon
Will not fade
We grew in faith
We fought and survived
Mother Rus for you Mother of God!

346   Dec 8   Colonna dell Immacolata
Four prophets defend
The Roman column rises
A hand to lift her skywards
The holy one unstained   Regard!
In heaven the blessed Mother.

347   Dec 9   Our Lady of Charity 2
The great aureole
Her golden cape
Her son in her arm
Mountains on the rim
The light of Charity rise.

348   Dec 10   Ancient British Saints 58
Gentle Caedmon   sing of God
Let us praise the Father of Glory
The Eternal Lord   wonders he gave
He first created the roof of heaven
Earth he made   for mankind dwelling.

349   Dec 11   Wisdomword 65

Better is the end than the beginning
Better is patience than pride
Don't let anger upset you
Anger forms a fool. Don't say
Yesterday you were better than today.

Mary for peace with Islam! ﷲ

350   Dec 12   Red Rose

Give me a rose, a red rose for love
Winter denies me
Close to the thorn, press close my dear
The bird sang life
A red rose flushed at the top of the tree.

351   Dec 13   Meaning of Icons 35

Meditate on the inner beauty
Her detachment from the world
Sorrowful she sees tomorrow
She knows the mercy he gives
He blesses her with his love.

352   Dec 14   Chamor

Are you a wild donkey
They were carrying sacks
I turn aside & crush your foot
Is that a foal or a colt
Why on earth is he riding on a jenny?

353   Dec 15   St Daniel the Stylite

Solid square tower 12 m high
Alone
Food by basket please
And po
I am the sufferer held in the sky.

354   Dec 16   Ancient British Saints 59

Forty days I fasted & blessed the place
The crypt of Mary Lastingham
Take the body and blood of Christ
Rest there awhile in spiritual peace
I spent a bright day among the nations.

355   Dec 17   Wisdomword 66

Wisdom overflows like the Pishon
Like the Tigris at time of first fruit
Like the Jordan at harvest time
Like the Nile instruction shines forth
Like the Gihon at time of vintage.

Mary for peace with Islam! الله

356   Dec 18   Star Aniseed

Put it straight in my pot
Wow was that hot
Threw it high
It stood in the sky
Rained down light showed a way.

357   Dec 19   Meaning of Icons 36

Every line signifies fullness
Observe how the himation
Fallen from his shoulder
Reveals the embroidered tunic
How brightly it shines with truth.

358   Dec 20   Piers Plowman 2
Truth tells us love is heavenly treacle
No sin in you if you use that spice
All of his works with love he wrought
Precious virtue he lered it Moses
Plant of peace, most heaven-resembling.

359   Dec 21   Buy a Hat
How about white, tall and pointy?
Or a top, like Fred Astaire?
Or unseasonal
Purple with a white lining
Santa Pixie hat or a God Jul Fairy?

360   Dec 22   Ancient British Saints 60
Heavenly song descended & ascended
The welcome guest who visits all of us
Now summons me to leave the world
No one knows the hour of their death
Let each make ready for their passing.

140

361   Dec 23   Wisdomword 67

The image of the invisible God
The firstborn of all creation
In him all things were created
Through him and for him
He himself is before all things.

362   Dec 24   Where's this? 27

Three candles hold a Xmas flame
The Arch swings up the censer
The people sing a blessed word
How bright the candelabra
Rejoice the birth of Jesus Christ!

363   Dec 25   Festivitas Natalis

All unaware on an afternoon
Music and laughter on the breeze
I peered over the precinct wall
A troupe of happy dancers
Leaping & calling in the joy of Jesus' birth.

364   Christmas 1
Did you hear what I heard
What was that
When the bébé started yelling
The roof started quaking
Sounded like a hundred wings.

365   Christmas 2
The moo cow took a good look
I kneel on the earth
Kissing thy foot
My gold is in the box
Your hand planted on my skull.

366   Christmas 3
Narrow frame a myrtle-wreath
Flowers and leaves and berries
Angels there with wings raised
Rotondo painted-table is a plate
Jesus born of Mary is the food.

367   Christmas 4
Look upon the good
Angels and prophets high
Joseph, Mary and infant Jesus
Holy kings pay homage
Don't look upon the crowd.

368   Christmas 5
The chiaroscuro of the mind
Out of the swirling half-hidden
Holy Virgin and son are in light
Faces of angels & philosophers
Stairs ascend beyond the world.

369   Dec 26   Bara Brith
What shall we give the babe in the manger?
Honey, and figs, and later green olives
And good Bara Brith baked at home
Mary thy milk the food that I long for
Wrap me in wool and sing me your song.

370   Dec 27   St Stephen Icon

Behold, I see the heavens opened up
The Son of Man standing at the right hand of God!
Holy St Stephen the Martyr pray for us
Swing the fragrant incense up to God
Let us share your vision of exalted Christ.

371   Dec 28   Piers Plowman 3

Heaven could not hold him   so heavy he were
He took flesh on earth   sorrow his fill
No leaf on the linden   was ever so light
Bright and piercing   as a needle point
Through stone and iron   he will go through.

372   Dec 29   Ancient British Saints 61

Owen threw himself upon the ground
Good Father what were those voices
They were angels calling me home
He departed the prison-house of flesh
His tomb is in Lichfield, a shrine of healing.

373   Dec 30   Ancient British Saints 62
Daughter of Holy Saxon kings
Thrown in a furnace she did not burn
On the stone she left her gentle footprint
She prayed & a demon quenched her flame
An angel restored it   pray for me, dear saint.

374   Dec 31   Ancient British Saints 63
Bede to bid command and pray
The land was filled with saints
Saints in Celtic   saints in English
Beloved islands blessed by Christ
Help me Father to write it down, amen.

375   Naoko 2
For all who read my verse
What it means to be alive
Within the walls
Do you know the words
Can you guess my glorious thoughts?

376   Biscuit Song

Tin of biscuits I will share them
Going halves   here you are
Lots remain   gone halves again
Now there's one   fifty-fifty
None remains   but *I love you* fills my tin.

377   Sunrise

Look at the dawn in the sky
You could say that is Jesus Christ
God the Father stands behind it
So where is his mother then?
Tell me that, where is the mother?

146

378   Four Angel Verses

1

Invisible messengers of heaven
Visiting the mind awaking
Air condensed by divine love
To be the word conceived salvation
Gabriel shimmers Hallo Goodbye.

2

Shall an angel assume a body?
Not from earth or water
How shall they disappear?
Not from fire, they would burn
Not from air which has no shape or color.

3

Those that see angels in imagination
A dream granted by heaven
Those to whom the angels appear as men
Three seen by Abraham
Raphael, one of seven, seen by Tobias.

4
Whether the angel shall have proper choice
Whose will must be the will of God
Pure flame of charity in heaven
On the wings of selfless love
To do the bidding of Eternal Love.

148

379   Maya

1

Long climb up the steps above Kobe
Eucharist in the dawn
Visiting friends I am here
Admiring the beautiful statue
母上 who's the little man in your belt?

2

Mary I'm still puzzling the task
To help them & love them
To live side by side
To support one another
To build compassion and peace.

3

Mon ami I will sit on your floor
I will sing in my breath
Repeating
感謝 感謝 感謝 聖母
You are good and kind I know.

4

There's more to say & do here
I must call on Paul
Advise me
So what did he say?
He said,   In love give them all.

5

How can I do such a crazy thing
Without restraint on love
Pray together
Power we know as Good
Grant that we may love each other.

6

Can I find you in the love
Can you find me in the love
Can I know in you the mercy
Can you know in me the mercy
The impossible is possible with love.

380 Saint Joseph at Dawn

In the hour before dawn we stand
A circle around Saint Joseph
The white of our wimple
Lanterns on posts
Awaiting dawn.

On the eastern hill
The sky fills with fire
Saint Joseph appears
He holds the child
How he lifts him up!

In a circle we stand
Mother lead us in Latin
We sing the sun up with joy
Father we thank you & bless you
Beloved sun you stand on the hill again.

381   Kimono

An old house stood up and spoke
A congregation in kimono
Holy sisters to wear native dress
We want Mary to show her love
The old family cloth is good for God.

A sister stood up and shouted
We love the ancient habits
Hallowed in form and tradition
Luxurious silken kimono? No!
We will not give up our holy habit!

Mother Teresa looked out of heaven
Long ago I'd have said the same
I refuse to wear the Hindu sari
Pagan cloth!   Jesus spoke
Wear the sari my daughter for God.

382 Final Profession

The flowers around the lectern
Sing for joy
Each to each rejoicing
Sister today is wed
Each repeats the happy word rejoice.

The wooden pillar of the altar
A carved tree with legs
Turned its head
And said
I'm holding up the living bread.

Alleluia gentle voices
Sister puts on strength
Her Beloved beside her
Fills her prayer with love
Pray for me dear sister.

383 Walsingham Procession

The younger walked in pilgrimage
Singing Ave Maria
They picnicked in the meadow
The older carried crosses
Banners and saints
Singing Salve
I was looking for Mary
I saw her
How young she was
She had long brown chestnut hair
Quick as thought
She was there with them
Then with us
Then we lost her
I ran along them looking
Merciful love forgiveness thy heart
Mary
Be with us
Let us be worthy.

384 The Ecumenical Covenant (Sept 2018)

The Ecumenical Covenant of The Shrine of Our Lady of Walsingham, signed by The Reverend Kevin Smith (Anglican Shrine) and Monsignor John Armitage (Roman Catholic Shrine) is an important statement of solidarity between the two Churches, promoting in unity the veneration and love of Mary the Blessed Virgin.

Walsingham is a holy meeting place, under the protection of Saint Mary, for Christians to grow in love with the Holy Mother, and each other, and to build a consciousness of love, healed in God in Christian faith.

Good news, good covenant!

(Sept 24 2018)

156

Poem Number and Note

1. Adapted from Proverbs 1.23. The poet prays for peace between Church & Islam.
2. 神 kō, god. 戸 be, door.
3. Adapted from Saint Thérèse of Lisieux, *L'histoire d'une ame* (p. 4). See poem 9.
4. Winter candle flames.
5. Saint John preserves the conversation of Mary & Jesus. Jn 2.1-5.
6. Series of 63 verses. Saints Theme. Celtic, British, Irish, Anglo-Saxon, Breton.
7. Adapted from Proverbs 6.6-9. Peace & love between Church & Islam.
8. Church of the Intercession (1165) Vladimir-Suzdal white-stone church.
9. Adapted from Saint Thérèse of Lisieux, *L'histoire d'une ame* (p. 4). See poem 3.
10. Tsubaki theme SM365.1.16, 20, 25; SM365.2.308; SM365.3.8; SM365.5.272, 275; SM365.6.10, 321.
11. Cyclamen persicum. Good snakes? See SM365.2.110; SM365.3.16; SM365.5.240.
12. The British Isles became Christian. Celtic and Anglo-Saxon saints.
13. Adapted from Proverbs 6.20-23. Peace & love between Church & Islam.
14. Filippino Lippi (c 1457-1504) *Adoration of the Christ Child*, Hermitage (c. 1480).
15. Adapted from Saint Thérèse of Lisieux, *L'histoire d'une ame* (p. 4).
16. *Wilton Diptych*. Saints present Richard II to Our Lady (c. 1395). Rededication of England in 2020.
17. Chimonanthus praecox. 蠟梅 Rōbai.
18. The early saints in Ireland and Britain.
19. Adapted from Proverbs 7.1-4. Peace & love between Church & Islam.
20. Inspired by *Maternità* (1899) by Mosè Bianchi (1840-1904) Ambrosiana, Milan.
21. Adapted from Saint Thérèse of Lisieux, *L'histoire d'une ame* (p. 13).
22. Inspired by Cathedral Saint-Malo. Stained glass (1968). Raymond Cornon (1908-1982).
23. School years a marathon. Read and learn Gospel Greek. Read LXX psalms.
24. Celtic Christian monasticism flowered in Ireland.
25. Adapted from Proverbs 8.1-7. Peace & love between Church & Islam.
26. Rogier Van der Weyden, *St Luke Drawing the Virgin* (1435-40) Museum of Fine Arts, Boston.
27. Her sister Pauline. Adapted from St Thérèse, *L'histoire d'une ame* (p. 17).
28. Swedish folk dress worn by Princess Victoria of Sweden.
29. Sitting cross-legged & praying is good. Pray with strength & joy.
30. St Columba, founder of Iona (c. 521-597) known as Columcille, Dove of the Church.
31. Adapted from Proverbs 8.8-11. Peace & love between Church & Islam.
32. Candles were blessed to ward off evil in ancient times (Feb 2).
33. Her father. Adapted from St Thérèse, *L'histoire d'une ame* (p. 18).
34. St Alphonsa (1910-1946) canonized 2008. St Mary's Ch. Bharananganam, Kerala.
35. No comment on this.
36. St Columba established continuity in traditions in Irish Celtic Christianity.
37. Adapted from Proverbs 8.13. Peace & love between Church & Islam.

38. Pierre-Auguste Renoir, *Portrait of Irène Cahen d'Anvers* [age 8] (1880).
39. A poor beggar. Adapted from St Thérèse, *L'histoire d'une ame* (p. 20).
40. St Colman's Cathedral, Cobh. Neo-gothic. St Colmán of Cloyne (530-606).
41. First published in *Saint Mary 100* first edition.
42. St Adomnan of Iona (624-704) also called Eunan. Negotiator.
43. Adapted from Proverbs 8.15-18. Peace & love between Church & Islam.
44. St Paul & Christ & considering the Sharon fruit. Persimmon. Is 35.1-2.
45. Her father. Adapted from St Thérèse, *L'histoire d'une ame* (p. 22).
46. Basilika Mariä Geburt (Birth of the Virgin Mary) (1157) Mariazell, Austria.
47. Puzzle for Japanese word suki 好き. See also *Hana 1* poems 53, 54, 103, 149.
48. The Holy Isle of Lindisfarne, a place for saints. Celts calling the English to heaven.
49. Adapted from Proverbs 8.22-26. Peace & love between Church & Islam.
50. Pierre-Auguste Renoir, *Two Sisters on the Terrace* (1881).
51. Adapted from Saint Thérèse of Lisieux, *L'histoire d'une ame* (p. 23).
52. Pope Benedict 16 visits Shrine & blesses a Benedictine Mother (Sept 7-9 2007).
53. Holy Trinity Cathedral, Riga. See SM365.1.144.
54. St Aidan of Lindisfarne (d. 651). Source from Bede (144-45).
55. Adapted from Proverbs 8.27-29. Rare Heb. word ḥūḡ (circle).
56. Isaac Fanous mosaic, Tekla Haymanot Church, Alexandria 1969.
57. With Father. Adapted from Saint Thérèse of Lisieux, *L'histoire d'une ame* (pp. 26-7).
58. Giotto. *Meeting at the Golden Gate* (1304-06) Cappella Scrovegni, Padua.
59. Imagining the presence of St Mary in Akashi, Hyogo.
60. St Cuthbert of Lindisfarne (c. 634-687). Trisagion Films YouTube was useful.
61. Adapted from Proverbs 8.30-31. Peace & love between Church & Islam.
62. Evdokia Adrianova told in a dream to go to Kolomenskoye to find holy icon (March 2 1917).
63. Her sister Marie. Adapted from St Thérèse, *L'histoire d'une ame* (p. 37).
64. Jan Gossaert, *Virgin and Child in a Landscape* (1531) Cleveland Museum of Art.
65. Inspired by a photo of Empress Kōjun (1903-2000) c. 1950. 香淳皇后.
66. St Cuthbert of Lindisfarne, wonder-worker, healer (c. 634-687).
67. Adapted from Proverbs 8.32-35. Peace & love between Church & Islam.
68. Lk 23.34. Jean Cocteau (1889-1963), Mural. Notre Dame de France Ch., London.
69. Adapted from Saint Thérèse of Lisieux, *L'histoire d'une ame* (p. 37).
70. Inspired by 吉永小百合 Yoshinaga Sayuri 『伊豆の踊子』 (1963).
71. Imagine the daffodil to be a statue of the saint.
72. St Cuthbert of Lindisfarne, wonder-worker, healer (c. 634-687). Source Bede (260).
73. Adapted from Proverbs 9.1-4. Peace & love between Church & Islam.
74. Beautiful stained glass gives rainbow light in Pontmain.
75. Adapted from Saint Thérèse of Lisieux, *L'histoire d'une ame* (p. 37).

76. Statue of female deity (c. 2500 BCE). Museum of Cycladic Art, Athens.
77. Hearing the magnified sounds of the flower's growth.
78. Durham Cathedral, the Shrine of Saint Cuthbert (c. 634-687).
79. Adapted from Proverbs 9.10-12. Peace & love between Church & Islam.
80. Lilium auratum. Golden-rayed lily, native to Japan. Also published in *Hana* 1.203.
81. Adapted from Saint Thérèse of Lisieux, *L'histoire d'une ame* (p. 41).
82. Stockless anchor used on a large ship.
83. Madonna del Popolo Icon, set in the Santa Maria del Popolo Basilica altar. Rome.
84. St Colman of Lindisfarne (d. 676) Synod of Whitby (663-4).
85. Adapted from Proverbs 10.1; 10.5-6. (using daughter in place of son).
86. Simone Martini (1284-1344) *Virgin of the Annunciation* (c 1333) Uffizi.
87. Adapted from Saint Thérèse of Lisieux, *L'histoire d'une ame* (p. 43).
88. "Bitter end" is the attachment of the anchor chain to the bulkhead.
89. Early 14th c. Wood. Rheinisches Landesmuseum Bonn.
90. British Celts flee the Saxon advance. Christian Church is established in Ireland.
91. Adapted from Proverbs 10.11-12; 29-31. See also 1 Pet 4.8.
92. Was it not taboo to reveal such things - because of the truth?
93. The true cross becomes the triumphant symbol of the Church.
94. Inspired by Russian Orthodox Icon, *Resurrection of Christ*, Holy Trinity Store, OCA.
95. Japan weather chart shows daily progress of cherry blossom & Momiji maple.
96. St Patrick of Ireland (c 390-461?). Patrick was a British Celt.
97. Adapted from Proverbs 11.11, 17, 19, 28, 30.
98. Isaac Fanous mosaic. St. Takla Haymanot Church, Alexandria (1969). Christ appears to saint.
99. Line misquoted from Alphonse de Lamartine, "Réflexion," "le temps est."
100. Orthodox Mission Kenya. Consecration of the second Bishop HG Neofitos Kongai. Videoclip.
101. Malus. Memories of home. Mother made crabapple jelly. See *Hana 1* poem 267.
102. St Patrick of Ireland (c 390-461?). Power in St Patrick's prayer.
103. Adapted from Proverbs 12.6,7,10, 12, 25. Peace & love between Church & Islam.
104. See also poems on sport in *SM365.6* and *Sport* 1 & 2.
105. His blood "to wash away sins." Adapted from *L'histoire d'une ame* (p. 54-5).
106. Forsythia suspensa. Named after William Forsyth (1737–1804), founding member RHS.
107. A series of three poems. Holy Mother Mary who teaches mercy.
108. St Patrick of Ireland (c 390-461?). Swift conversions of kings and their courts.
109. Adapted from Proverbs 13.1, 9, 10, 14, 24. Peace & love between Church & Islam.
110. Roman Basilica. Popolo door pediment early renaissance art-work c. 1470.
111. Adapted from Saint Thérèse of Lisieux, *L'histoire d'une ame* (p. 55).
112. Inspired by Newsletter 2016 OSC Mission BC Canada.
113. To be truly faithful we must love one another.

114. St Brendan the Navigator (c. 484-577), also called Brendan of Clonfert.
115. Adapted from Proverbs 14.1, 2, 3, 21, 22.
116. Apparition of Mary, Santuario Santa Maria delle Grazie, Spezzano Albanese (CS).
117. Adapted from Saint Thérèse of Lisieux, *L'histoire d'une ame* (p. 57).
118. クララ Kurara. Sophora flavescens. Food for Shijimiaeoides divinus.
119. To love one another we must find one another lovable.
120. St Brigid of Ireland, Bridget of Kildare (d. 524). Saint Brigid Cathedral.
121. Adapted from Proverbs 15.8, 9, 13, 16. Peace & love between Church & Islam.
122. Gerard David (c. 1455-1523) *Virgin with the Milk Soup*. Musées Royaux des Beaux-Arts.
123. With sister Céline. *Imitation of Christ* 3.43.4. Adapted from *L'histoire d'une ame* (p. 57).
124. Cnoc a' Chalmain, Hill of the Dove, House of Prayer, Iona. April 29, 2018.
125. Shall he not much more clothe you? (Mt 6.28-31).
126. Saint Ailbe (6th c.) (Saint Elvis) Irish saint. Legend.
127. Adapted from Proverbs 15.19, 20, 24, 30. Peace & love between Church & Islam.
128. Shrine and Statue in Harissa (650m), overlooking the Mediterranean.
129. Adapted from Saint Thérèse of Lisieux, *L'histoire d'une ame* (p. 71).
130. Adapted from Simon King's article in *Nature's Home* (Spring 2017).
131. Vision given to Fr. George Nasis, Annunciation Ch., New York, Grk Orth. (May 3).
132. Celtic Crosses. Clonmacnoise Monastery, Ireland founded c. 550 by St Ciaran.
133. Adapted from Proverbs 15.20, 23, 26. Peace & love between Church & Islam.
134. Said to have health benefits. Not recommended, except for sheep.
135. Adapted from Saint Thérèse of Lisieux, *L'histoire d'une ame* (pp. 73-4).
136. Two beautiful Cathedrals in San Francisco. Attending both in one day.
137. Black Madonna carved statue (c. 1330). Our Lady of Bavaria (May 14).
138. Legend assoc. with St Ciaran founder of Clonmacnoise, Ireland.
139. Adapted from Proverbs 15.33; 18.12; 22.4. See also Lk 1.52.
140. Sisters from Japan gave me a coaster embroidered with an unusual design.
141. Adapted from Saint Thérèse of Lisieux, *L'histoire d'une ame* (p. 74).
142. Valaam Icon of the Mother of God. Natalia Andreyevna's deposition 7 Aug. 1897. OCA website.
143. Commiphora myrrha.
144. Clonmacnoise Monastery, Ireland.
145. Adapted from Proverbs 16.1, 3, 33. Peace & love between Church & Islam.
146. Our Lady of Help for Christians. Callao, Lima, Peru Festival May.
147. With Pope Leo XIII. Adapted from *L'histoire d'une ame* (p. 77).
148. Our Lady of Help for Christians. Breña, Lima, Peru Festival May.
149. The Venerable Bede (673-735). Tomb in Durham Cathedral. Feast day May 25.
150. Clonmacnoise. Irish monastic civilization flourishes and blesses the nation.
151. Adapted from Proverbs 16.15, 24. Peace & love between Church & Islam.

152. Mosaic in Redemptoris Mater Chapel, Vatican by Fr. Marko Ivan Rupnik (1999).
153. With Pope Leo XIII. Adapted from *L'histoire d'une ame* (p. 78).
154. Circle of Gerard David (c. 1455-1523). Museu Nacional de Arte Antiga, Lisboa.
155. My dear mother. Natalia Andreyevna's deposition 7 Aug. 1897. OCA Aug 7. See SM365.2.39.
156. Responding to Seamus Heaney (1939-2013), "St Kevin and the Blackbird."
157. Adapted from Prov. 17.17, 22; 18.4, 24. 18.24: Heb. to love aheb trans. as friend.
158. *Valaam Icon of the Mother of God*. Father Alipy. 1878. OCA website. Aug 7.
159. Carmelite saint. Adapted from *L'histoire d'une ame* (p. 81).
160. Holy Icon of the Mother of God of Igor (Prince of Kiev) OCA website June 5.
161. Inspired by Polish dance team "Lublin" in Ourense, Galicia 20090503. SM365.6.238.
162. Inspired by OSC Mission BC Canada Newsletter 2016.
163. Adapted from Proverbs 18.10, 15, 16. Peace & love between Church & Islam.
164. Neomys fodiens. Highly developed sense of smell.
165. Adapted from Saint Thérèse of Lisieux, *L'histoire d'une ame* (p. 81).
166. Inspired by the Scottish sword dance.
167. Unexpected icon found in a newspaper advert.
168. St Kevin (Caoimhin) of Glendalough (d. 618).
169. Adapted from Proverbs 19.8, 11, 17. Peace & love between Church & Islam.
170. Commelina communis. Used to dye cloth blue. See SM365.4.173.
171. Adapted from Saint Thérèse of Lisieux, *L'histoire d'une ame* (p. 82).
172. Inspired by the Scottish sword dance.
173. Arisaema urashima.
174. St Columbanus (543-615) Irish founded monastery Luxeuil (Acts 2.44-46 & 4.32).
175. Adapted from Prov. 20.7, 27. Verse 27 meaning extended in line 3. Heb. nîr lamp.
176. The Book of Kells (c 800) Detail folio 309r. A peacock perches (Jn 6.38).
177. Adapted from Saint Thérèse of Lisieux, *L'histoire d'une ame* (p. 86).
178. The soul dances joyfully.
179. Butterfly Shijimiaeoides divinus. オオルリシジミ. Aso, Kyushu.
180. St Finbar (Fionnbahrr) (c. 560-610) Patron saint of Cork.
181. Adapted from Proverbs 22.1, 4, 9. Peace & love between Church & Islam.
182. The Book of Kells is a holy masterpiece. See the Chi-Rho page. Folio 34r.
183. Adapted from Saint Thérèse of Lisieux, *L'histoire d'une ame* (p. 87).
184. 時計草 Passiflora caerulea.
185. Patisserie artist candy sculptor. See *Hana 1* poem 219.
186. Saint Kentigern d. 612 (called Mungo), patron saint of Glasgow. Feast Jan 13-14.
187. Adapted from Proverbs 23.12, 15, 16.
188. The Irish Monastic tradition produced a unique Celtic masterpiece.
189. Sister Pauline. Adapted from St Thérèse, *L'histoire d'une ame* (p. 89).

190. 時計草 Passiflora caerulea.
191. Candy sculptor, stall artist. Festival in downtown Shanghai.
192. St David of Wales (c. 542-601). Llanddewi Brefi Village & Church.
193. Adapted from Proverbs 24.30-34. Peace & love between Church & Islam.
194. Inspired by Peruvian folkdance Asociación Cultural Qhaswa Minho Festival 20120829.
195. Her father. Adapted from St Thérèse, *L'histoire d'une ame* (p. 90).
196. 時計草 Passiflora caerulea.
197. "Mother 風の門 kaze no mon" 北海道江別市・原田ミドー作 Harada Midō (2001).
198. St Dympna, martyr (d. c. 650). Healer of insanity.
199. Adapted from Proverbs 25.21-22. Lines 3-4 added. Cp Mt 5.44-5; Rom 12.20.
200. Inspired by Peruvian folkdance group Qhaswa at Minho Festival 20120829.
201. Adapted from Saint Thérèse of Lisieux, *L'histoire d'une ame* (p. 94).
202. Inspired by Irish Fairy Reel with three circles of dancers (Lincoln Irish Dancers).
203. Habenaria dentata. See article on Botanyboy.org website. See also SM365.1.213.
204. St Winifred of Wales, Winefride (d. c. 650) Holy Well.
205. Adapted from Proverbs 27.1, 2, 19. Peace & love between Church & Islam.
206. Inspired by Asociación Cultural Qhaswa dance at Minho Festival 20120829.
207. Adapted from Saint Thérèse of Lisieux, *L'histoire d'une ame* (p. 98).
208. Puhtitsa Monastery Estonia video clip with BVM in the vault.
209. Also called the Dakota or C-47, first true passenger airliner. Still in use – 80 years.
210. St Dyfrig (Dubricius) (c. 465-550). See Tennyson, "Dubric the high saint."
211. Adapted from Proverbs 27.14, 17, 18. Peace & love between Church & Islam.
212. Indian Saint. Saint Alphonsa the Healer. Franciscan Clarist. Feast 28 July.
213. Adapted from *L'histoire d'une ame* (p. 99). (This occurred on BVM nativity Sept 8).
214. Medellin flower festival, Colombia. Silleta, great bouquet carried on back.
215. Also called the Dakota or C-47, first true passenger airliner. Still in use – 80 years.
216. St Illtud (c. 6th c.) Abbot of a monastery. See name, Llanilltud Fawr.
217. Adapted from Proverbs 29.3, 11, 18, 23, 25. [Female pronoun used.]
218. Éire postage stamp rcvd from OSC. Fireworks Anemone. Pachycerianthus multiplicatus.
219. Adapted from Saint Thérèse of Lisieux, *L'histoire d'une ame* (p. 111).
220. Japanese lanterns. Imagined a Festival parade for St Mary in Macao or Sao Paulo or Nagasaki.
221. Dancing Mayim on a boat on Lake Galilee.
222. St Teilo (c. 6th c.) tomb in Llandaff cathedral. See name, Llandeilo Fawr.
223. Quoted from Proverbs 30.4. Peace & love between Church & Islam.
224. Sanctuaire de Querrien, Bretagne, France. Pardon (festival) August 15.
225. 1 Kgs 7.19. Flowers and fruit were used in temple ornamentation.
226. Inspired by "The Transitus of Saint Clare" Franciscan text.
227. 800 years! Holy procession of Saint Clare in Malaga 20120811 [YouTube].

228. St Brannoc of Braunton, Devon (6th c?) a holy well.
229. Adapted from Proverbs 30.24-28. Peace & love between Church & Islam.
230. Prayer that healing be given to the faithful at Walsingham Well, amen.
231. Francesco Botticini *Assumption of the Virgin* (1475-6). National Gallery, London.
232. Mountain associated with Basque goddess Mari, veneration transferred to St Mary.
233. Ilex latifolia. Leaves used for messages in ancient Japan.
234. British Celts flee to Cornwall to escape the Saxons.
235. Adapted from Proverbs 30.29-31. Peace & love between Church & Islam.
236. An unusual dream. Lithops, called "living stones."
237. Adapted from Saint Thérèse of Lisieux, *L'histoire d'une ame* (p. 117).
238. Ceratonia siliqua. A man rests in the shade of the carob.
239. Imagine a duty for a Poor Clare Capuchinas, part-work as Clini-clown, and nun.
240. St Piran of Cornwall (c. 6th c.), patron of tin miners.
241. Adapted from Proverbs 31.10-11. Peace & love between Church & Islam.
242. Embroidery icon made by OSC, TMD North Wales. E. & W. unite in prayer.
243. Prov. 9.4; Is. 66.12-13. Adapted from *L'histoire d'une ame* (p. 117).
244. Fight bad information saying goodness is false. Seize truth. Jesus & Mary are Love.
245. Inspired by Newsletter 34, Sisters of St Clare, Saginaw (Jun 2016). Lk 9.51.
246. St Petroc (d. c. 564). Cornish saints in place names. St Petroc's Church, Bodmin.
247. Adapted from Proverbs 31.12-13. Peace & love between Church & Islam.
248. Paper Lantern Festival, Montelupo Fiorentino (Florence) (St Mary Nativity Sept 8).
249. Adapted from Saint Thérèse of Lisieux, *L'histoire d'une ame* (pp. 127-8).
250. 1969 *Something Beautiful for God*. Dir. Peter Chafer. Presenter Malcolm Muggeridge.
251. (1233-1251). Source *The Franciscan Book of Saints*, ed. Marion Habig. Feast Sept 4.
252. St Germoe (6th c?). Patron of Germoe Church. Companion of St Breage.
253. Adapted from Proverbs 31.14-15. Peace & love between Church & Islam.
254. Melkite Christians hid sacred cave (Lebanon). Rediscovered 1721. Feast Sept 8. See SM365.1.254.
255. Adapted from Saint Thérèse of Lisieux, *L'histoire d'une ame* (p. 147).
256. Peruvian & Chilean folk music Inca panpipes. Carlos Carmelo (YouTube).
257. Inspired by *Ancient Chinese Verse*. DVD9.8. (『新漢詩紀行』石川忠久監修)
258. St Breaca (6th c?). Companion of St Germoe, patron of Breage Church.
259. Adapted from Proverbs 31.16-17. Peace & love between Church & Islam.
260. Butterfly Shijimiaeoides divinus. オオルリシジミ. Aso, Kyushu.
261. Adapted from St Thérèse of Lisieux, *L'histoire* (p. 153). Song of Songs 1.3-4.
262. Drone flying over the Akita harvest towards Our Lady of Akita, Garden of Mary.
263. Borassus flabellifer also called Toddy Palm. Fruit juice.
264. Cornish place names & saints. Cury is Corentin, Breton. St Corantyn Church.
265. Adapted from Proverbs 31.18-19. Peace & love between Church & Islam.

266. Children dancing. Sr Maria Goretti Lee SPC canonical visit Indonesia May 2017.
267. Dream-vision of Carmelite sisters. Adapted from *L'histoire d'une ame* (pp. 160-1).
268. Scene from a Nepalese village. Hulling the rice.
269. Kalimantan. Villager dances in honor of the visit of the SPC sisters May 2017.
270. British princess flee to Brittany (c. 5-6th c) Christian faith. Sen Synt Sans Sant Naomh.
271. Adapted from Proverbs 31.20-21. Peace & love between Church & Islam.
272. A vineyard in Tunisian hills. Muscat wine made from ancient times. St Augustine.
273. Adapted from Saint Thérèse of Lisieux, *L'histoire d'une ame* (p. 163). 1 Cor 12.31.
274. Sweet potatoes & yams on both sides of the Pacific.
275. Banjarbaru novitiates dance wearing white. SPC visit sisters May 2017.
276. St Malo (c. 550) founder of St Malo Cathedral. (Saint Vincent of Saragossa Saint-Malo).
277. Adapted from Proverbs 31.21-24. Peace & love between Church & Islam.
278. In celebration of Sr A. OSC TMD Oct 1 2016. Jer. 46.18; Song 7.5; Is. 35.2.
279. Sourced from L. Ouspensky, *Meaning of Icons* (SVS Press 1982: 48-49).
280. Potatoes and sweet potatoes (patata and batata). Peru and Chile.
281. Lev 23.40. See Menachem Posner, "Why can't I use a lemon instead of an etrog?" (citron). Chabad.org.
282. St Patern (c. 500). Patron Saint-Patern Church, Vannes. Procession banners.
283. Adapted from Proverbs 31.25-27. Peace & love between Church & Islam.
284. Sr Marie Adele Brise encounters St Mary (1859). Words adapted from website OLGH Champion.
285. Sourced from L. Ouspensky, *Meaning of Icons* (SVS Press 1982: 63-64).
286. Our Lady of Akita at harvest-time.
287. Sister Marie Adele Brise (1831-1896). National Shrine, Champion, Wisconsin.
288. St Corentin (c. 450). Patron Quimper Cathedral. Beautiful spires.
289. Adapted from Proverbs 31.31. Peace & love between Church & Islam.
290. Sister Marie Adele Brise encountered Saint Mary (1859). Champion, Wisconsin.
291. Saints, angels, patriarchs & Blessed Mother pray before Christ. (Ousp. 63-64).
292. Pilgrims walk to Our Lady Shrine, Champion, WI (21 miles).
293. Walk to support Catholic education. Our Lady of Good Help, Champion, WI.
294. St Pol Aurélien (c. 500) Patron of the town Saint-Pol-de-Léon.
295. Adapted from Tobit 4.3-4. Peace & love between Church & Islam.
296. St Peter of Alcantara (1499-1562) meeting (1560) St Teresa of Avila (1515-1582).
297. Adapted from L. Ouspensky, *Meaning of Icons* (SVS Press 1982: 69).
298. Miagao Church, Iloilo, Philippines (Unesco). See SM365.8 for Philippine theme.
299. Nyiur is Malay for Coconut. Tagalog: Niyog. Polynesian: Niu. Pacific fruit.
300. St Pol Aurélien (c. 500). Magnificent Cathedral in Saint-Pol-de-Léon.
301. Adapted from Tobit 4.7-9. Peace & love between Church & Islam.
302. Polynesian myths about the coconut.
303. Sourced from Ouspensky, *Meaning of Icons* (77). Isaiah 7.14. See SM365.6.335.

304. Poet remembers window in Duke Humfrey library, Bodleian, Oxford.
305. Mt 10.5; Lk 9.52; Lk 10.33; Jn 4.9; Jn 4.39.
306. St Brieuc (Brioc) (c. 500) first Bishop of Saint Brieuc. Holy Fountain & Cathedral.
307. Adapted from Tobit 4.14-16. Peace & love between Church & Islam.
308. Hanging up daikon radish for pickling in late autumn.
309. Sourced from L. Ouspensky, *Meaning of Icons* (81). See SM365.1.331 & 2.27.
310. Oils and resins ancient treasures.
311. See Ex 15.20.
312. St Tugdual (c. 500) first Bishop. Founder of Tréguier Cathedral.
313. Adapted from Tobit 4.18-19. Peace & love between Church & Islam.
314. Inspired by Filadelfia Church West Kalimantan girls dancing for Christ (YouTube).
315. Smolensk Icon. Sourced from Ouspensky, *Meaning of Icons* (81-84).
316. Where is heaven? I asked him and he said
317. Puzzling on the name, Saint Jerome be praised.
318. St Samson (c. 550) of Dol-de-Bretagne. Magnificent Cathedral. Two ancient wells.
319. Adapted from Tobit 12.6. Peace & love between Church & Islam.
320. 5 Josephs: Arimathea; Hymnographer (c 850); Volokolamsk (c 1470); Calasanz (c 1600); Cupertino.
321. Tichvine Icon. Sourced from Ouspensky, *Meaning of Icons* (83-85).
322. 東京ゲートブリッジ. Tokyo Gate Bridge. Tokyo Olympics 2020.
323. This is not about the name but it is important. What is the reference?
324. St Augustine of Canterbury (d. 605) converts King Ethelbert c 597.
325. Adapted from Tobit 12.7. Peace & love between Church & Islam.
326. Traditional Nigerian method for extracting palm oil. Women's work.
327. Kazan Icon. Sourced from Ouspensky, *Meaning of Icons* (87-88).
328. Akashi Kaikyō Bridge 明石海峡大橋 Akashi Pearl Bridge.
329. "Mary" is a holy name, thanks be to God, amen.
330. St. Ethelbert (c 560-616) king of Kent, Christian Frankish wife Bertha.
331. Adapted from Tobit 12.17-18. Peace & love between Church & Islam.
332. Manual oil-press for extracting palm oil in Nigeria.
333. Mother of God Enthroned Icon. See Ouspensky (89-90). See SM365.2.15.
334. Nagasaki bridge (1634) built by monk Mokusu, Kofukuji Temple 黙子如定 (1597-1657).
335. Gen 1.10; Num 12.10; Isa 23.6; Ps 24.2.
336. "Holy Heaven's king," quote from "The Rune Poem." Pray for us St. Ethelbert.
337. Adapted from Tobit 13.10-11. Peace & love between Church & Islam.
338. The statue found floating in the sea of Nipe Bay, Cuba (1612).
339. Eleousa Icon. Umileniye. See Ouspensky, *Meaning* (92-93).
340. A sister in kimono visits a church member and prays a blessing on her house.
341. Puzzling on 聖母 seibo Holy Mother.

342. St Hilda of Whitby (614-80). Synod of Whitby 664. Renowned for wisdom.
343. Quoted from Ecclesiastes 1.9-10. NRSV. Peace & love between Church & Islam.
344. A flower for the winter solstice. Flower native to Mexico.
345. Vladimir Icon. See Ouspensky (96). See other Vladimir icon poems SM365.5.3 etc.
346. The Column of the Immaculate Conception, Piazza Mignanelli, Rome (1857).
347. Statue of Mary in Minor Basilica of El Cobre, Cuba.
348. St Caedmon (d. 680) poet monk in Whitby Abbey. Adapted from Caedmon's Hymn.
349. Adapted from Ecclesiastes 7.8-10. Peace & love between Church & Islam.
350. Responding to Oscar Wilde, "The Nightingale and the Rose."
351. Tolga Icon. See Ouspensky, *Meaning* (97). See SM365.2.32.
352. Gen 16.12; 42.27; 49.11; Num 22.23-25; Mk 11.1-7; Mt 21.1-7; Lk 19.29-35; Jn 12.14-15.
353. St Daniel the Stylite (d. 490) & see Stylite Tower Umm ar-Rasas, Jordan.
354. St Cedd the evangelist (c. 620–664) brother of Saint Chad.
355. Sirach 24.25-27. Peace & love between Church & Islam.
356. Illicium verum.
357. Korsun Icon. See Ouspensky, *Meaning* (100). See SM365.6.286.
358. Lered: taught. AVC Schmidt B-Text 1.148-52. See SM365.6.358.
359. 蛍袋 Hotarubukuro. Campanula punctata. Bellflower. (Flowers July).
360. St Chad (Ceadda) Bp of Lichfield (c. 634-672). Source from Bede (207-212).
361. Col 1.15-17; Prov 8; Sir 24; Gen 1.26.
362. Archbp Alexios. Christmas, St Porphyrios Grk Orth. Church, Gaza City. 20170107.
363. Inspired by performance YouTube 長崎県南島原市有馬小学校 Shimabara, Arima.
364. Inspired by Fra Angelico, *Nativity*, Fresco in San Marco (cell #5) (c. 1440).
365. Gentile da Fabriano, *Adoration of the Magi* (1423). Florence, Galleria degli Uffizi.
366. Masaccio, *Birth Salver Depicting the Nativity* (1427-8). Berlin, Staatliche Museen.
367. Lorenzo Monaco, *Adoration of the Magi* (1422). Florence, Galleria degli Uffizi.
368. Leonardo da Vinci, (unfinished) *Adoration* (1481-2). Florence, Galleria degli Uffizi.
369. Inspired by Christmas song by Sr An. OSC TMD Wales (2015).
370. St Stephen the Protomartyr. Acts 7.56.
371. Verses adapted from *Piers Plowman*. AVC Schmidt B-Text 1.153-59.
372. St Chad (Ceadda) Bp of Lichfield (c. 634-672). Source from Bede (207-212).
373. St Mildred, Abbess of Minster-in-Thanet, Kent (d. c. 725).
374. St Bede (673-735) *A History of the English Church and People*.
375. Responding to Horie Naoko 堀江菜穂子 (1994-) published *Ikite ite koso*, 2017.
376. Adapted in response to poem by Horie Naoko, "Takusan no Bisketto."
377. Thanks be for mercy. In the sunrise the resurrection of life.
378. Aquinas, *Summa Theologica* I.50-64. 7 angels attend on Him.
379.1 Haha-ue (Mother). See Tōri Tenjō-ji Temple Statue of Maya, mother of Gautama.

379.2 Visiting Tōri Tenjō-ji 切利天上寺 also called Mayazan Tenjō-ji 仏母摩耶山天上寺.
379.3 To build equilibrium and peace in Japan.
379.4 To build a loving knowledge about one another.
379.5 To defend and support one another.
379.6 To deepen love and wisdom in both of us.
380. Inspired by a photo-essay by Sr. J-M. M. PCPA OSC OLS Monastery AZ.
381.1 Roots in the culture, love for the old family, support of old forms.
381.2 Learn from the history & meaning of sisters' European religious costume.
381.3 Jesus told her directly to wear poor native clothing (1949). Defend traditions (2020).
382. Sister A. final profession on Saint Teresa of Avila 2016 TMD PCC OSC.
383. In commemoration of the Covenant signed Sept 24 2018. Our Lady of Walsingham.
384. May love grow stronger between the English Churches, amen.

Profile

Stean Anthony

I'm British, based in Japan. I've written a series of books of poetry promoting understanding and peace. Find out more from the list at the end of this book. I have also published *Eco-Friendly Japan*, Eihosha, Tokyo (2008). *Monday Songs 1-5,* and *Eitanka 1* (pdf file textbook freely available on website – and sound files). Thanks to Yamaguchi MK for kind help.

New Projects
Japan Angels 2 (haiku verses on Japanese themes)
Hagios Paulos 4 (verses on the theme of Saint Paul)
Enarchae (vol 3 in the story of Phim, Holy Land episodes)
Sport 2 (poems on the theme of sport)
Hana 2 (poems on the theme of flowers and other topics)
Saint Mark 450 (the Gospel in short verses in Japanese)

Author's profits from this publication to be divided between leading Churches of respective Christian denominations in Kobe city area, including all Orthodox, Catholic, and Protestant Churches, with some gifts of love to other Churches and faiths (in particular, peace with Islam).

> Lord God
> Hear my
> Prayer.
> May all Christians in all churches give
> A gift of love to one another.
> May the
> Wounds of
> History
> Be healed
> At last.
> Lower
> The barriers
> And link us up,
> Through Jesus Christ. Amen.

Word of Blessing

A blessing of peace
Be with us
And between us
In the spirit of love
People of every faith.

In all things
Thanks be to God.
Amen.

Stean Anthony Books with Yamaguchi Shoten. Original poetry & translations & adaptations. Most are textbooks.

- *Selections from Shakespeare 1-5* (selected passages)
- *Great China 1-4* (translations of classical Chinese poetry)
- *Kŏngzĭ 136* (poems based on the sayings of Confucius)
- *Manyōshū 365* (translations of ancient Japanese poems)
- *One Hundred Poems* (inspired by 百人一首 *Hyakunin Isshu*)
- *Heiankyō 1* (translations of ancient Japanese poems)
- *Inorijuzu* (Buddhist & Christian words for peace)
- *Sufisongs* (poems for peace in Jerusalem)
- *Soulsongs* (poems for peace in Jerusalem)
- *Pashsongs* (songs & poems by Stean Anthony)
- *Bird* (poems on the theme of birds)
- *Sport* (poems on the theme of sport)
- *Hana 1* (poems on the theme of flowers)
- *Japan Angels* (poems on Japanese themes)
- *Songs 365* (poems based on the Psalms)
- *Songs 365* (Japanese translation)
- *Songs for Islam* (poems based on verses in the Koran)
- *Isaiah Isaiah Bright Voice* (poems inspired by Bk of Isaiah)
- *Saint Paul 200* (poetic phrases from the *Letters of Paul*)
- *Hagios Paulos 1-3* (poetry based on life & letters of St Paul)
- *Gospel 365* (based on the Synoptic Gospels)
- *Saint John 550* (poetic version of the Gospel of St John)

- *Saint John 391* (translation to Japanese of *Saint John 550*)
- *Saint John 190* (transl. to Japanese of *Saint John 550* Catholic Letters)
- *Saint Matthew 331* (poetic version of Gospel of St Matthew)
- *Saint Luke 132* (chaps 1-2 in Japanese verse *"Mary's Gospel"*)
- *Saint Mary 100* (poems dedicated to St Mary)
- *Saint Mary 365 Books 1-6* (calendar of poems on themes relating to Mary, Holy Mother, flowers, icons, prayer, scripture)

- *Messages to My Mother 1-7* (essays on faith and other things)
- *Mozzicone 1-2* (essays about questions of faith & other things)
- *Monday Songs 1-7* (pdf textbooks of English songs)
- *Eitanka 1* (pdf textbook teaching poetry)
- *Psalms in English* (75+ lectures in English teaching the Psalms pdf textbook). Pdf are freely available.
- *Piesat Course 1-3 Lectures on English Poetry* (pdf text files)

- *Exnihil* (story written in short paragraphs)
- *Bərešitbara* (story written in short paragraphs)

SAINT MARY 365 Book 7
　(聖母に捧詩365節)
by Stean Anthony

Company : Yamaguchi Shoten
Address : 4-2 Kamihate-cho, Kitashirakawa
　　　　　Sakyo-ku, Kyoto, 606-8252
　　　　　Japan
Tel. 075-781-6121
Fax. 075-705-2003

SAINT MARY 365 Book 7
　(聖母に捧詩365節)　　　　　定価　本体2,000円(税別)

2019年12月20日　初　版
　　　　　著　者　　Stean　Anthony
　　　　　発行者　　山 口 ケ イ コ
　　　　　印刷所　　大村印刷株式会社
　　　　　発行所　　株式会社　山口書店
〒606-8252京都市左京区北白川上終町4-2
　　TEL：075-781-6121　FAX：075-705-2003
　　　　出張所電話　福岡092-713-8575

ISBN 978-4-8411-0945-0　C1182
©2019 Stean Anthony